BLACK GIRL therapy

THE NOVEL

AISHA HOLLAND DUDLEY & TRE FLOYD

Black Girl Therapy
©Copyright 2023 Aisha Holland Dudley & Tre Floyd

Tre Productions

4913 West Street
Forest Park, Georgia 30297
www.trefloyd.com
(404) 600-2981

Cover design & edits: Christine Racheal, **Airris Books**
www.airrisbooks.com

Cover photo: The Red Brand

CONTENTS

PREFACE

Every girl has a number. What's yours? You may have a single digit. You could even select a combination of numbers. Regardless, it is my belief that a girl can't know who she is until she knows her number. It's a part of the process—a girl's journey to self-acceptance. It is at that point that she can decide whether to work on herself, or not. To pursue a future better than her history, or not. To heal from her brokenness, or not.

The 18 girls you are about to meet are real, and these stories happen every day. You may find yourself in a similar season; or your sister, your bestie, or even your mother, could be facing situations like the ones you will read in the next few pages.

None of these girls are alone, and neither are you. Some of them are challenged with trauma from their past. Some of them are dealing with drama in their present. And some are simply afraid of what the future holds.

Last year, I set out to meet 18 Black girls of varying ages and backgrounds. We would meet one-on-one at my favorite spot. To start, I would simply ask each of them two questions: 1) What is your number? 2)What is your story? I documented these conversations and put them into each chapter of the book you are about to read. These are their stories. I didn't add or take anything away. I merely formatted their stories into chapters. Each of them found telling their story therapeutic, and I hope you find healing in reading them.

To keep their identities secret, I've removed their names and only identify them as their selected numbers. Each number explains who they are and, before you finish reading, I hope you find your own.

CHAPTER 1

GIRL 999: PAST TRAUMA

I believe I'll go by girl 999. I once read that 999 means that a current situation will come to an end for new opportunities to present themselves. However, in order to have new opportunities, one must deal with their past—no matter how traumatic it might be. Past trauma makes it hard to see right in front of me some days. I've held on to so much baggage that I can't move forward unless I first release something. I'm ready to turn a new leaf, but in order to get there, I know I need therapy.

It is easy to assume that those raised in a two-parent household have better lives and become better people than those who do not. Well, that's simply not my truth. Two-parent households normally do pretty well financially, but that's only if they are both willing to work and take care of the children.

My mom carried us, and my father did what he wanted, which rarely included working. Christmas gifts were wonderful if we got them. We learned to be grateful for a present on our birthdays. And back-to-school clothes were exciting, but rare.

Whenever our father had money, he would go out and waste it. Whether it was drugs, alcohol, or women, he would pick one of his many vices to blow his money on while Mom struggled to keep a roof over our heads. We grew up poor. Poorer than poor. We were so poor that we used baking soda to brush our teeth. I could handle being poor, but the financial strain was nothing compared to the abuse.

Weekly, I would watch my father start a fight with my mom while he was drunk or high. As the oldest, I would stay tucked in my room to make sure that my siblings were okay. I was 6 years older than my sister, and 8 years older than my brother, so I witnessed the abuse for years before they came along. If I could prevent them from being traumatized, I would.

One day, my sister was in a Little Miss pageant. My dad claimed the dress she wore was too provocative for her age. It was a typical, floor-length church dress, and nothing was showing, but he wanted to pick a fight. I hid my siblings in the closet, gave them Rice Krispy Treats, and put headphones on their heads as our parents quarreled. They had no idea that on the other side of the door our dad was beating the brakes off our mom.

I wanted to help so badly, but I was too small. Mom told me that whenever he came home like that, the best help I could offer was to get myself and my siblings out of the way. So, that's what I did. I had no headphones, so I could hear every slap against her face, the thud of her body against the floor, and imagine every bruise darkening throughout her skin. They yelled and screamed at each other for a while, and then I heard a loud *thump*. Afterwards it was silent.

I waited until I heard my dad's truck crank up and leave before I went to check on Mom. He had beaten her until she passed out. That day, I'd had enough, so I called the police. By the time they arrived, Mom was awake, but she told them she had fallen. The police knew it was a lie, but they couldn't do anything unless she was willing to file charges. I loved my mom so much, but I could not understand why she wouldn't file charges against him.

And then there was April 17th. I won the school science fair and my mom had cooked an amazing meal to celebrate. We had black eyed peas, cornbread, fried chicken, and yams. She knew they were my favorite dishes. When my dad arrived, we were already eating at the table. He was having one of his spells, as I would call them. He immediately started to argue about something stupid, which led to a fight.

This day was different though. I guess mom had had enough too. She was known to fight back, but this time, she was giving it all she had. They fought so hard that they ripped off each other's clothes. I didn't have time to grab my siblings and hide. As a young kid, how do you handle seeing this? I was too young to break it up, so all I could do was watch and cry. My favorite meal would never be the same. I never wanted that meal again. I wished I had never won the science fair. Even several years after marriage would pass before I prepared that meal for myself. It always reminds me of that day.

My siblings and I have never discussed the violence in our home. It's as if it never happened. They were so young. I often wonder how much of it they remember.

And I'm curious to know if they struggle with it as much as I do.

As I grew older, I realized that I hated my father. I even thought of ways to kill him, but I never went through with it. Maybe I should have. As my sister grew older, she decided not to get married. Many guys have asked, but she chooses to remain single. She says that she enjoys her independence. That may be true, but a part of me believes she fears her marriage would be as toxic as our parents' relationship.

My brother is an alcoholic. He knows it but he won't go to rehab. He was young, but he knows *something* happened, although he can't quite remember. Therefore, he drinks and tries to put the pieces together in his own way. All of this could have been avoided if Mom had just left.

Why did my mom not hate my father? Maybe she did. How could she still love him? Maybe she didn't. Did she ever think about killing him? I bet she did. I know she had other options, but maybe she couldn't see them clear enough.

My sister doesn't talk to Mom as much as I do. I believe she saw our mother as weak, but she was the strongest woman I ever knew. Perhaps she fought our father so that we weren't the recipients of his blows. She was his punching bag so that we didn't have to be. It took many years for me to come to such conclusions, but my sister would never accept it.

So much of this childhood trauma affects me in my adult life. I find myself severely guarded because of the things I witnessed as a child and a teenager. I was blessed to find a wonderful husband. He has never raised his hand at me. However, I shudder when my husband even raises his voice at our child, but I could never explain it to him. I don't want him to know about the trauma that I faced as a child.

To be honest, it took me a long time to even get married. I would date and date, but always found a reason to break up. I dated several decent guys but seemed to find something wrong with each of them. It took me a while to realize that I consistently compared the men to my father. I guess I had that in common with my sister. My own insecurities spoke for me, but I didn't realize it.

Once, my husband spanked our son. It was the day of the father-daughter dance at school, and I was so happy. I had never been to a father-daughter dance, and I was excited for my daughter. I had finished curling my daughter's hair, and my husband had just gotten ready, when my oldest son walked into the room. He wanted his dad to take him to the video game store, but his dad didn't have time before the dance. His dad said he would take him the next day, but that wasn't good enough for our son. He said he hated our damn family and attempted to storm off to his room. Before my husband realized it, he popped him. My son probably deserved it but, in that moment, when my husband's hand struck my son, all I could see was my father hitting my mother. I screamed. I believe it scared my husband and son as they both rushed over. I told them it was nothing and that I was fine, but I was crying my eyes out.

My son said, "Mom, I'm sorry. I know I was disrespectful. I didn't mean it."

My husband told me he knew it was much deeper for me than him disciplining the kids, but he didn't know the depth of my trauma. He said, "I'm going to take our baby to the dance, and we'll talk tonight."

I always knew that I should go to therapy to work out issues that stem from childhood trauma, but I would talk myself out of it every time. Going to therapy would mean that the day would come for me to open up and explain what really happened to me. I've worked hard keep it in my past and hidden from my husband and close friends. Would they judge me? Would they think differently of me? Would my husband question the woman he married?

That night, when my husband came home from the dance, I decided to tell him about my childhood. He just held me. He didn't judge me, and he didn't say anything. He held me all night. This one silent action said everything I needed to hear. I no longer had to bear the weight of my burden alone.

A few years back, I lost my father, but not before sharing that I had forgiven him. Whether he knew what I was forgiving him for or not, it really didn't matter. I forgave him for all the trauma he caused me and my siblings. I forgave him for the trauma that he continued to cause, and I forgave him for not refusing to care about the scars he'd left behind. Forgiveness didn't heal all my wounds. It didn't make it right, and it didn't help me to forget, but it gave me a chance to move forward. It gave me a chance to leave the past behind and to grow in every area of my relationships moving forward.

My siblings decided against attending our father's funeral, and I couldn't be mad at them. I sat on the front row with my husband and our children. When I looked over at my daughter and could sense how much she admired her dad, I shed a tear. There was no sadness for my dad, but gratitude for that moment. I was grateful that she would never endure the trauma I experienced and that she has a father who loves her.

I then looked over at my mom. She sat and cried. It was a different type of cry. It was sorrowful as if she was sad her husband was gone, but it was also peppered with joy as if she was glad. It was a cry of solace, and a cry of endurance. She felt relief. I wondered if she regretted her decisions. I held her hand for a while and, through her hand, I could feel her soul. It was full of thought, remorse, and regret. I think that if she could do it all over again, she would.

I thought of my mother's relationship with her own father. She never mentioned him. Was he like my dad? Did her dad beat Grandma? Was the behavior normal for her? I didn't know and I didn't care to ask. I just held her hand and hugged her, so that she knew I loved her, and that everything was well.

The Luther Vandross song, "Dance with My Father," comes to mind. While many girls wish to dance with their father again, I'm glad I don't have to deal with mine again. I'm ready to turn a new leaf. I'm ready to move forward with my life, forward with my family, and forward without the trauma of my past. First, I need therapy.

Chapter One Reflection

Is there trauma from your past that you have intentionally suppressed? What are you afraid for others to discover about you?

_____

_____

_____

_____

_____

_____

_____

How are you dealing with (or have dealt with) traumatic experiences from your past, and how have you moved forward?

_____

_____

_____

_____

_____

_____

_____

CHAPTER 2
GIRL 69: SEXUALLY FREE

Thursday, it was Ronnie. Friday, I believe his name was Terrance. Saturday was a blur. And Sunday, I think it was Kim and Irvin. All I know is that I woke up naked in a hotel, and that there was a note on the dresser that said, "We had a great time. Checkout is at 12."

My number is 69, and it needs no further explanation. Basically, I love sex. I'm not a prostitute. I don't get paid for it, although I could. I just enjoy it. Thrusts, yanks, screams, exhales, the moment of climax, are all not-so-guilty pleasures of mine. My number could've been *infinity* because, honestly, I don't know how many I've bodied to date. I usually add one or two a week, and I'm not ashamed. However, I also can't keep piling bodies on bodies. And I can't keep pressing my luck not knowing where I might wake up. I need therapy.

Every weekend, I meet someone new. Some of them audition for the role of my man, but I already know the deal when I meet them. I'm never actually casting, but a sneak peek would do. I have one thought, and one thought only, in mind. *I'm going to fuck you, and we will never speak again.*

Only a few have made it to round two. Every now and then, I go for a third round but that's usually my limit. I've tried having a regular, but it never pans out.

Either they try to cuff me, or I see myself catching feelings, and no one has time for that. I just enjoy sex with men... and occasionally a woman.

If I were a dude, no one would think anything of it. They would say I'm just "being a man," and one day I'd settle down. So, why can't women be the same way? I'm just trying to catch a nut like the next nigga. I don't consider myself a whore. I don't think I'm nasty, and I have never engaged in sexual intercourse for money. If I'm a whore, then most of your daddies are whores. Why can't women be as sexually liberated as men? I simply enjoy going out, having a good time, meeting a guy, and jumping his bones. If they say *no*, then I back off. I don't sleep with married men (unless I don't know they're married), and I don't do porn. I have a reputation to protect, and a great career to prioritize. I have some wild stories though. Whew, the places I've done it and the people I've done it with!

I like to meet guys at public bars, preferably on well-lit streets. Some people are crazy, so you can never be too safe. You won't find me on the rough side of town, and I don't do clubs in dark alleys. My favorite spot is Bar Tex, a little spot in Midtown where you can find a fine brother with a little edge. That was my type. I don't like guys that are too hood because they're crazy and can't let go. I don't like guys that are too lame, because they don't have the best sex. They usually have the best equipment but don't know how to use it. So, my mission is to find one that's just right—something in between.

I've had a lot of great sex, but I think my best round was with Daryl and Ronnie. I remember the night I met

Daryl and Ronnie. Daryl approached first and tried to get my number.

He asked, "Can I take you on a date? You're so beautiful."

"Do you have a wife?" I responded.

"No."

I asked if he had to wake up early in the morning, and he said *no* to that too. That was all I needed to know.

I told him, "Why don't we skip the date and go to the hotel across the street? You're horny. I'm horny. There's no need to buy me dinner when we both want what's between the other's legs." That turned Daryl on. It was refreshing to meet a woman who was so open.

He told me the night was young, and that we should have a few more drinks before heading over to the room. Besides, he wanted to finish watching the game. I wasn't opposed to that. In the back of my mind, I thought, "If it ain't good, I'm leaving you in the room and coming back to find someone else anyway."

We had a few shots and swapped random stories. As it turns out, he was an ex-NBA player, which explained why he was so invested in the game. He only played a few years due to an injury and he'd had quite a few sexual experiences himself. While he shared some of his fantasies, I shared some of my realities, and we laughed and talked for a while.

He confidently expressed all he desired to do to me that night. "You ain't gone do shit," I thought.

Since we were both so free-willed, he believed we should do something wild, and I was down.

"What about a threesome?" he asked.

"Threesome? That's the best you can do?"

"Look, we can make it a whole orgy if you're down."

"It gets less entertaining after four, unless you're into voyeurism...which I'm not."

"You like to get all the attention, huh."

"Not necessarily. I like to be *in* the game and not watching it."

"What shall we do? We can go by the sex store first."

"I got all the toys we need." I laughed.

Daryl was a cool guy. The game ended and I ordered another round of shots. We were about to leave when a guy walked over. Perhaps he didn't realize I was talking to Daryl, or he didn't care. But he calmly asked if he could get me a drink. Me being me, I didn't owe anyone anything. Daryl didn't have my loyalty, just my attention.

"Sure," I said. I could tell Daryl was jealous.

"I'm Ronnie."

"Nice to meet you, Ronnie. This is Daryl."

"Oh, my bad. Is this your dude? I didn't mean any disrespect."

"He's not my dude."

I could tell Daryl felt some type of way. "You're dropping me for this guy?"

"I haven't dropped anyone. I'm just sitting at the bar having drinks."

"Then are you ready to go?" Daryl asked.

"Where are you off to so soon?" Ronnie chimed in.

I started to say that we were going to a hotel to fuck, but upon a second thought, I wanted to see just how far I could go.

"Well Ronnie, Daryl and I just met. We've been drinking for hours, and we're going across the street to fuck."

It caught Ronnie off guard. "Oh! Well, don't let me stop you."

"Oh, you couldn't stop me, but you're a handsome guy. I would fuck you."

I think Ronnie liked the idea that I seemed to choose him over Daryl, and right in Daryl's face. He said, "Is that right? Well, you and I can go to that hotel instead."

"I don't know. You see, Daryl and I have exchanged stories, and he's a bit of a freak. I think his sex might be better."

"I'm willing to bet my stories are better."

"Well, let's have a few more rounds," I suggested.

Daryl, Ronnie, and I sat at the bar and drank some more. At first, there was tension between the guys. It was a battle of the egos, and the winner would be the man came with me to the room that night. However, after a few pours of tequila, they didn't know what was what, and didn't care. They slapped a high fives like a few high schoolers. Thankfully, I could hold my liquor. I was buzzed but nowhere near drunk.

Then Ronnie asked, "Y'all ever did X?"

I wasn't big on drugs, but I admitted to trying it before.

"Not in a while," Daryl responded.

I don't know why, but we decided to pop one and head out.

After ingesting XTC, we went across the street to the hotel. The effects of the pill hadn't kicked in, so we sat at the bar in the hotel lobby and had another round. It was at that moment that I realized I was the only female. Was I about to have a threesome with two *men*? They were both fine, and I wasn't against it, but some guys have an issue with that. They were so drunk and high that they barely knew what was going on.

We went up to the room, and before I could even get my clothes off, these niggas were already butt ass naked. They fucked me in every position and on every piece of furniture. We even did it on the balcony. It was obvious that the men were extremely intoxicated when Daryl slapped Ronnie's ass because he thought it was mine.

After a few hours, we fell asleep. I awoke first, got dressed, and left. I can only imagine what happened when those two woke up in bed together butt ass naked. I wish I were a fly on the wall. They were so high that neither of them will remember what happened. I never saw them again, but if I do, I will definitely go for round two.

You may be wondering if I ever date, and I do. I am one of the few ladies who knows how to separate intimacy and sex. When I'm with my guys, or tricks (as some may call them), I have sex. I'm often judged, especially by married women. I'm frequently called a *bitch*, or a man stealer, but I don't try to take anyone's man. If a man wants me and he's attached, that's between him and his woman. I don't owe anyone anything.

If we're being honest, every woman has some 69 in her. They may not let it out, but it's there. There's no way any woman can tell me she's never walked into a bar, restaurant, or even a church, saw a fine man, and said to herself, "I'd fuck the hell out of him!" Even if she didn't do it, I'm sure that if she thought no one would judge her, she would.

This isn't my first time in therapy. I also went to a few sessions when I was a little girl. That therapist would say that I'm this way because of my uncle. We credit him for stealing my innocence. It hurt the first time he penetrated me, but I got used to it. I even told my mother when it happened. I think she believed me, but nothing was ever done about it. Police were never called, and she told me to never tell anyone.

A few years ago, he was killed. Apparently, someone else's mother wasn't as passive as mine. Therapists say

I'm promiscuous because I explored sex at such a young age, but I don't think so. I just like it. If my uncle had never touched me, I would still be the same way. Right? There's no connection for me. The guy and I are both there for mutual pleasure. I don't often use my name, and I prefer not to know theirs. It keeps things uninvolved and simple. You come in, we fuck, you say you had a good time, and you leave. That, my dear, is sex.

I'm not like most women. I can separate sex from intimacy. When I'm in a relationship, it's more intimate. We make love. There's foreplay. There's kissing. There's gazing into each other's eyes. I enjoy intimacy, but I don't want it with everyone. It's a good thing that guys don't always want intimacy. They want sex, and I have some of the best sex out there.

Since I'm so comfortable in my own skin and very pleased with my incredible sex life, many will probably wonder why I need counseling. Well, I'm afraid that sex will kill me. Between catching an STD, waking up next to someone I don't recognize, and jealous niggas, someone or something is going to kill me. Despite my fear, I just can't seem to stop piling up bodies. I need therapy.

Chapter Two Reflection

Girl 69 mentions that she can separate sex from intimacy. Do you believe this is possible for women? Is random sex acceptable? Are feelings only involved when there is intimacy?

_____

_____

_____

_____

_____

_____

_____

_____

Do you have a Girl 69 within you? Have you ever explored it? Why or why not?

_____

_____

_____

_____

_____

_____

_____

_____

CHAPTER 3

GIRL 777: CHURCH HURT

Call me 777. That's for the threefold, perfect trinity. It goes without saying that I love the Lord. There has been nothing more meaningful in my life than the relationship I've had with the Lord, Jesus Christ. He radiates through every part of me, and there isn't a day that goes by that I don't stop to give him praise.

I was the poster child for Greater Life Baptist Church. I went to church all day on Sundays. We would start at 9 AM for Sunday school, and then would shift to noon day service before moving into the evening program, and then night service. On Monday, there was choir rehearsal; Tuesday was for prayer service; Wednesday was for Bible study; Thursday was for the youth choir rehearsal; Friday night service was for us to receive God's word; and then there was Saturday morning prayer. I had been in this cycle since I was a child, so it didn't bother me. It was the norm. Church was my entire life, and I loved my life. That was until my life was shattered by the church.

I should have left the church a long time ago, but it was all I knew. It was safe, and I'd made friends with my comfort zone. I believed everything Pastor said, so I can't blame it all on him; but after 20-plus years of going to church 7 days a week, I need therapy.

As I reflect, I believe my issues are rooted in my youth. In Sunday school, I was so curious and would have many questions. My teacher, Sister Higgins, told us that God created Heaven and earth. I asked, "When did God create dinosaurs, and did they eat people?"

As a 5-year-old, these were real questions, but instead of giving me a real answer, Sister Higgins would say, "Don't you question God." Then she would tell my parents that I was acting out in class. From these occurrences, I learned to shut my mouth and never question God's word.

During his sermons, Pastor would say that if a woman wore short skirts, she wasn't saved. Women also couldn't wear heavy make-up, pants, or "flashy" jewelry. I didn't understand why women had so many rules, but men didn't have any. I was also told that Halloween was of the devil. This one really hurt because classmates and neighbors would get dressed up as their favorite characters, and I couldn't. Pastor said it was ungodly. Although he never explained what made it so ungodly, my parents said to listen to the Man of God. Therefore, I never went trick-or-treating. Since I was always in church, I met most of my friends there, so they were in church too. Mom said we had to be set apart from the world.

My first date was high school prom. I went with Daniel Stevens. His dad was a deacon, and his mom sang in the choir. I'd had a crush on him for a while, so when Mom gave us her blessing to go to prom, I was so excited.

On prom night, I didn't dance much. They only played worldly music, and I wasn't used to that type of atmosphere—loud, thumping music, young people grinding on each other on the dance floor, and I swore some of them were drunk, but I didn't know how they could've gotten it.

Despite the shenanigans, Daniel was a perfect gentleman. After prom, he drove me home and kissed me slightly on the lips. He asked if I would be his girlfriend. No guy had ever asked me out before. I was flattered, but unfortunately, Dad was waiting up for me and got a glimpse of the kiss. He was not happy about it and forbade me from seeing Daniel again. I cried until graduation.

My college campus was not far from home, so I was able to go to church on the weekends. College life took some getting used to; there were so many people from so many backgrounds. I had to consistently remind myself to set myself apart even in moments that I wanted to be liked or wanted others to know that I was kind-natured and cool. It wasn't always easy, but I remained focus.

My parents didn't like my roommate. They said she was the devil, but I thought she was fun. I even went to my first college party with her. When I didn't have anything to wear, she dressed me in her clothes—a short, red dress. At first, I said I couldn't wear it, but she insisted that God had given me my shape and I needed to show it off.

The party was off campus. I noticed some familiar faces, but none of them knew who I was until that night. It was as if I was someone totally different. Girls actually spoke to me, and guys asked me for my number. It was new territory and so unfamiliar to me, but I liked the attention.

The next day, I went shopping with my roommate. It was time I switched up my style. I didn't buy ridiculously short skirts, but I decided to dress *my* age and not my mom's age. Who knew that changing a wardrobe would be so liberating?

The following night, I decided to watch a Harry Potter movie. I'd always wanted to but was told that it was satanic. After watching, I thought to myself, "Who made up these rules?" It was just a movie. I found myself trying all kinds of things I had never had a chance to because of church. I didn't see myself as a sinner; I just did what I was told I couldn't—and without reason. The love I once had for the church was transformed into a love for enjoying life.

I didn't go out *every* week, but sometimes I would. I hadn't had sex yet, but I was definitely becoming more and more curious. One night, I went to a bar and ran into an old church member. He didn't recognize me in my new attire. I was having a Shirley Temple when he walked up and asked, "Can I get you another drink?"

I turned to him and said, "No, Deacon James, I'm good."

"Deacon James? You know me?"

It was then that I realized he had no clue who I was, and I could smell the alcohol on his breath. I said, "You know me from church."

"Oh! You're looking like a grown woman. How old are you now?"

"I'll be 19 in a few days."

"Well, you *are* grown. Tell me…are you feeling yourself yet?"

"Umm…I don't know what you mean."

"You know. You got a boyfriend?"

"No, I don't?"

"Need a sugar daddy?"

At that moment, I realized Deacon James was flirting with me. "Deacon…"

"Call me Willie."

"Okay, Willie. I think you've had enough."

"Maybe I have. Will you walk me to my car?"

"Sure."

I grabbed my purse and walked him out. When we got to his car, he insisted he take me home. I said I was good and that my roommate had come to the bar with me.

He said, "No good church girl should be out so late," and continued to insist that he take me home.

I called my roommate and told her that I would accept his ride, and she said she'd see me in the morning.

When we pulled up to my apartment, I thanked Deacon James for the ride, but when said he had to use the bathroom, I had no choice but to invite him inside.

"You mind if I have a seat for a moment? Can I get something to drink?"

I figured he just needed to sober up a bit, so I grabbed a couple of Cokes from the fridge for us to drink.

"Here, come sit by me."

"Okay." I moved closer to him.

"You smell so good."

"Thank you, Deacon."

"I told you to call me Willie."

"Thank you, Willie. It's getting late."

"Yeah, it is. It's warm in here too. Don't you think?" He began to unbutton his shirt.

"What are you doing?"

"Just getting comfortable. Tell me. Have you ever been with a man?"

"Do you mean have sex?"

"Make love. Come over here."

"I'm waiting for marriage to make love."

"You need to be ready for your husband. Come let me show you how."

"I don't think that's what God had in mind."

"Shhh. I'm older and more experienced. I know what God wants. The Bible says to listen to your elders. Now come sit by me."

I wasn't sure what I should do, but I was a young, and he was an attractive man. I didn't want to disappoint God; the Bible clearly speaks of obeying elders. So, I sat next to him.

Before I knew it, Deacon James had taken my virginity. He was gentle, but I was confused. Something was wrong. When he was done, he kissed my forehead and said not to speak of it to anyone. I cried myself to sleep that night.

Church the following week was awkward. Deacon James acted as if he didn't know me. I sang on the praise team as I usually had, and afterwards, I went home. That night, I had the worst cramps ever. I didn't know what was wrong. I woke my roommate from her sleep and begged her to take me to the emergency room.

At the hospital, the doctor asked if I could be pregnant. It had never crossed my mind. What if I was pregnant? What if I was having Deacon James' baby? I knew I would be shunned from the church. I told the doctor *no*. He ran some tests and gave me something for the pain.

A few days later, the hospital called with my results. I wasn't pregnant, but I had an STD. I knew exactly where it had come from, and I was pissed—beyond disgusted. *Did he know? Had he done it on purpose?*

I decided to pay Deacon James a visit. I went to his house, and to my surprise, a woman came to the door. I asked if Deacon James was there, and she asked what I needed with her husband. Husband? I never knew Deacon James was married. Everything within me crumbled. I told her it was personal.

"If you're looking for money, look somewhere else."

"What?"

"Look, we paid the last girl, and we ain't paying no one else," she said, and then slammed the door in my face.

I was intrigued by this *last girl*. Had he slept with someone else from church?

A conversation I once overheard about Tamera Jenkins came to mind. A few ladies in church said she was a whore and slept around with married men. She was a few years older than I was, and she no longer attended church.

I decided to visit Tamera, who lived in an apartment not far from campus. She came to the door with a baby on her hip. When I asked if I could come in, she hesitantly obliged.

"Why did you leave the church?"

"I love God, but church ain't all glitter and gold," she replied.

"What do you mean?"

"Everyone ain't saved like they say they are."

"Did you sleep with someone at church?"

"Why?"

"Because I did."

"He got you too, huh?"

"Who?"

"Deacon James."

"How did you know?"

"You look like his type—young, naive, innocent. Just like I was."

"Wait, is he…?"

"Yeah, it's his baby."

"Did you tell anyone?"

"I told my parents, but they didn't believe me. They said to close my mouth like I should've closed my legs."

"So, he's paying you."

"Paying me? No, why you say that?"

"I went by his house, and his wife said they paid the *last girl*."

"Then there must be someone else."

"Another one? You think it's someone from church?"

"Hell yeah. Men like him have a pattern. Let's think about who else distanced themselves from church."

It came to me in an instant. "Oh my God! Christin!"

I hadn't talked to Christin in years, and I hoped she still had the same number. Thankfully, when I called, she answered. I asked if we could meet up, and she agreed.

After telling Christin about my ordeal, she admitted that she had also slept with Deacon James, but assured me that he hadn't paid her any money. Her relationship with him was the reason she had to move away. She told her parents, but they never told her uncle, Pastor Williams. We decided then that Pastor had to learn about the actions of his trusted deacon.

The three of us went to the church. Alone, I asked Pastor if we could meet in his study. He agreed under the condition that First Lady could come as well so that we wouldn't be alone. Once I entered his office, I told Christin and Tamara to come inside. Pastor's demeanor changed instantly. I told him that something serious had happened.

"I don't want to hear it," he said.

"Pastor, you must. This could ruin the church."

"If you are here to tell me about your indecencies, I don't want to hear it. I thought you were a nice, wholesome, young lady. When did you start running with whores?"

"These are not whores. We are children of God, and your deacon has taken advantage of us. There could be more."

"Save it."

"I'm not lying. First Lady, as a woman, you must listen to us!"

"Pastor, will you let us have your office for a moment?" First Lady said.

When he left, and it was just us women, First Lady said, "As a woman, there will be things we must endure. Did Deacon James touch you?"

"Yes," I responded. "He also touched Tamara and Christin, your own niece."

"Have you told anyone?" We all shook our heads. "Then you must not. These are matters of the church and not of the law. God will handle Deacon James."

"But Auntie, he touched me!"

"He does a lot of good for the church. Aren't you willing to sacrifice for the Lord?"

"Sacrifice? Would God want me to sacrifice my virginity?"

"Calm down, child. It will be okay."

"Wait. You knew?" Tamera asked.

"Knew what?"

"You knew he was messing with her. Christin is your niece, and there's no way you didn't know what was happening. Wait…" Tamera paused a moment. "It's you! He's paying off the church for y'all to keep quiet."

"Nonsense."

"How many others are there? You don't even know, do you? I hope you burn in hell!"

"Well spoken by the homewrecker who had a baby with a married man."

"I was raped! We were all raped by a predator that you and this church protect! Let's go, girls. She'd rather be kept in fine clothing and have her title than put a predator in jail. Not me. I'm going to the police."

We went to the police. After their investigation, we discovered that Deacon James had raped 13 other girls, and it was finally time for him to be brought to justice. The church stood beside him the entire trial. My parents even stopped talking to me for a while because they said I was trying to bring the church down.

These days, I'm not a church-goer, but I continue to pray, and I still love God wholeheartedly. My spiritual connection is deeper now that it's truly based on love and not on the rules of man. I may return to the fellowship of a church one day, but as of now, I'm still church hurt.

I realize how much the church caused me to miss out on as a child. I grew up fearful because I thought any and everything would send me straight into a fiery hell. I was so naïve and became easy prey to a predator because I was never exposed to the concept of sex and consensual interactions. I would never raise my child in such a manner. I tried to pray away all the church hurt, but prayer alone isn't working. My God, I need therapy.

Chapter Three Reflection

Have you ever felt church hurt? Where are you now in your healing process? What has been the most challenging part?

_____

_____

_____

_____

_____

_____

_____

_____

In your opinion, has "the church" done more harm than good in society? Why or why not?

_____

_____

_____

_____

_____

_____

_____

CHAPTER 4
GIRL 411: BITTER

I'm 411. I have all the info you need about men. In short, all they do is mess you up. When I say *mess you up*, I mean fuck you up so bad that you can't stand them. Men will leave you so bitter that you can't see a good thing staring you in the face. And so bitter that your only goal becomes turning everyone against them.

What's worse is not even realizing how much your own bitterness is hurting you emotionally and physically. It kills your soul. No woman would ever admit it because that would mean that *he* won. I'll be damned if I let him win. And for that reason, I won't be caught dead in therapy. I would rather wallow in my bitterness and pretend to be happy by my damn self. Who the hell am I fooling? Everyone around me knows I need therapy. If I'm honest with myself, I know it too.

My extreme disappointment in men started when I was about 22. I was a recent college grad starting my career at a new firm when I met a guy at work. I was the newest marketing agent and still decorating my office when I heard a baritone voice say, "You have a package."

"Just leave it on the desk," I said without turning to look at him.

"If you could, sign here."

His request annoyed me; I was trying to hang a painting on the wall, and it disrupted my progress. When I turned around, he stood there—arms bulging from his collared shirt, shining beard, and with skin that had the essence Jamaica and made use of the best oils. As I scanned his body from head to toe, I noticed that the package in his hand wasn't the only one he was carrying. I walked over and signed the document to keep myself from staring.

"There you are. Thank you," I said.

"Can I help you with that?"

"With what?"

"The painting you were trying to hang."

"I guess I could use a hand. Just be careful."

"You must be new."

"I am. I'm the new marketing agent. My plan—to be VP of the urban division in 4 years."

"I don't think we have an urban division."

"We don't. I plan to start it."

"Oh, that's what's up, career woman." He extended his hand to me. "I'm Eric, a courier here. I'm mostly on the 9th floor."

"Nice to meet you."

"Hope I'm not being too forward, but would you like to grab lunch?"

I wanted to grab more than lunch. "I can't. I have some work to finish up here. Maybe some other time."

"Sounds good. I'm sure I'll see you around."

"Definitely."

He left. On one hand, I could've stared at him and caught my drool in a cup for hours on end; but on the other hand, I couldn't be seen with a mail courier, especially not if I wanted to be taken seriously at the firm. Not to mention I didn't have time for a relationship. My college sweetheart and I had only recently called it quits when I realized he was opting for the "no end in sight" degree track. I just wanted to focus. Besides, I had all the man I needed in the nightstand.

Despite my lack of interest, Eric always found a reason to stop by my office. I didn't want to date him, nor did I have time, but I couldn't ignore the fact that he was handsome.

One day, I was working late, and Eric was still in the building. When he came to my floor to drop off a package, he noticed that I was still there and offered to wait until I was in my car before he left. It was sweet that he wanted to ensure I was safe. I told him I was a big girl, but he said he would feel much better if I at least gave him my number and called when I made it home safely. It was a decent strategy to get my number, and I knew that's just what it was, but I couldn't refuse such a kind gesture.

I worked a few more hours that evening, and decided to text him when I got home. We went back and forth for about a half hour—just small talk, but it was obvious that a friendship was developing.

About a week later, your girl was horny, and my bedside buddy wasn't doing it. I wanted to text him, but I knew it wasn't wise. I thought it would be best to go out and meet someone new. Just as I got dressed, Eric texted me. He said that although I'd rejected him a million times, he had tickets to a show and really wanted me to join him. So, I finally agreed to go on a date with him.

That night, we saw Chante Moore, who I love, but there's no way he could've known that. And to my surprise, he could actually hold a conversation and was a gentleman. If any man could be a total package, Eric would also be wrapped in glitter and bows. He was a genuinely good guy.

After we decided to go steady, I kept it professional at work and didn't tell anyone. I told him how much I needed to prioritize my goals, but that we could share when the time was right.

After a few months together, we knew that it had gotten serious. I wanted him to excel in his career, and he wanted me to excel as well. We decided to move in together to cut expenses so that Eric could leave his courier role and focus on finishing his degree.

The plan was going well until we were about two years in, and I found out I was pregnant. Pregnancy was eye-opening. I thought Eric would be a good father, but I had to make sure my baby was taken care of financially. It was imperative for Eric to return to work since we had a baby on the way, and he didn't complain. He received a paid internship at a company he was really interested in working for when he finished his degree. He even took on a part-time job at night…or so I thought.

One day, I started digging into my finances and realized that Eric is nothing more than a con artist. I had an incredible amount of debt, my savings was practically gone, and many of my credit cards were maxed out. How could I have been so stupid? Had he been using me the entire time? Was this his play from the beginning?

We argued throughout my entire pregnancy. A journey that was supposed to be beautiful was tainted with spite. On several occasions I wanted to put him out and be done with it, but Eric had charm that worked on me every time. This nigga, who had maxed out my cards and ran through my money, was still pulling the wool over my eyes. He had a way with words that could make a fish buy sand at a beach. I'm ashamed to admit it, but he kept feeding me false promises and I took the bait time after time. First, he claimed the money was spent on investments and said we were going to cash out within a few years, and then he claimed it was for tuition payments. It was always something.

After I had the baby, Eric still worked his night job. One night, the baby became ill while staying over at my mom's. She was vomiting, and although my mom insisted that she was fine, she suggested that I come get her. I looked at the clock and saw that it was almost time for Eric to get off, so I called to see if he would swing by my mom's. I knew his job wasn't far from my mom's house, so when he didn't answer, I decided to swing by after I picked up the baby.

It was then that I discovered he hadn't worked there for months. His ex-boss said he was fired because he never showed up at work. I was furious. That was it! Where was this nigga going every night?

I decided to say nothing, but I was going to look through his phone. He knew I wasn't the snooping type, so he wouldn't be smart enough to delete anything. They say if you go looking for something be prepared to find it, and sure enough, this nigga had been fucking at least three different girls over the past few months. We fought that night, and he begged and pleaded for me to let him stay. He admitted he was wrong and promised not to do it again because he desperately wanted—no, needed—his family. This nigga even said he wanted us to go to church together. I wanted to leave so badly, but I stayed.

Years went by and Eric never graduated. The debt piled up, and I was forced to sell my house and downsize. After the sale, I finally put Eric out. However, we had a child together, so he was still in my life to some extent. I would be lying if I didn't say that I still had a soft spot for him and admit that we slept together from time to time. He was basically my safety dick. With a small child, I didn't have time to meet new guys, report to a full-time job, *and* trying to get out of debt. So, when I needed some, I would call him, and he would handle it.

Years went by and I found less and less time for me. One day, as I walked through my house, I paused in front of the mirror. Where I used to see this young, vibrant, ambitious woman, I now saw an oversized, middle-aged woman. Before Eric, I would never leave the house without being fully put together. My hair was unkempt. My ends weren't clipped. I wore an old maid's gown, or duster, as my grandma calls it. Before, it wasn't worthy lounge apparel, but there I was. Who was this woman?

As I stood there, I received a text from Eric. He said he was sorry that he couldn't make it over the previous night, but he was free to pull up that evening. Was I really a second-place chick who couldn't even get a dick appointment? I removed my gown as I stood in front of the mirror and looked at myself. Skin that used to glow had become dull. My body no longer had the *bang* of a 20-year-old. I began to cry. What had happened to me? It was at that moment that I knew I was done with Eric.

When I realized I was getting old and needed to get back to me, I started to date again. At the same time, I also realized how bitter I had become. I hated Eric, and it came off like I hated all men. I went on a date or two, but the men said they couldn't see me again until I was completely over my ex. I thought I was over *him*, but that I just wasn't over all he had put me through.

One guy said he thought I had potential to be a great woman, but he couldn't fix the hold that Eric had on me. After that guy, I stopped dating. I thought men were dumb. They just didn't know how to handle me, and I wasn't about to let another Eric use me again. I even instilled it in my daughter and placed great emphasis on never letting a man have the upper hand. She'll probably need therapy one day too.

More years went by, and my daughter grew up, but I was still alone. No one asked me on dates anymore—not that I would even say *yes*. I am even older now and still bitter. How could I allow this to happen to me? He took the best part of me. He stole something that I can never get back. He stole my youth and left me with resentment.

Now I'm in my 40s, bitter, and no one wants me because of it. I can't be too mad at Eric though. As much as he stole, I allowed him to do it—over and over again. Year after year, I let him strip me of my youth.

If anyone asks, I say I'm happy alone, but we all know the truth. If I'm ever going to find happiness again, I'm going to need therapy first.

Chapter Four Reflection

In what ways have previous bad experiences or bitterness caused you to miss out on something?

_____

_____

_____

_____

_____

_____

_____

_____

CHAPTER 5
GIRL 9: SPRUNG

Call me girl 9. Here's why: I met this brother, and I felt so high that I was on cloud 9. I'm still not sure what came over me. When I first saw him, I turned into a teenage girl—all smiles and giggles—and it worsened when he smiled back. Our exchange would have been fine…if I didn't have Jeff, my husband. And let's not forget the two children we share at home. Now I'm caught between the hubby and gym bae. I need therapy.

Jeff and I have been married for 12 years. He has an amazing job which allows me to stay home and take care of our two beautiful children. Jeff is a phenomenal provider, but that's not all he is. He's smart, handsome, and has a cool lameness about him—like Randall on *This is Us*, which means he's quite lame but doesn't quite know it. I think it's charming.

I love Jeff. Sex is good, but after 12 years and 2 kids, we don't do it like we have in the past. However, it's still good when we get to it. Jeff was all the man I needed…until Dante crossed my path.

I'm in the gym 3 to 5 days a week. I try to squeeze in an hour after I drop the kids off at school and before Jeff gets home from work. Aside from the obvious health benefits, it helps me relieve stress. Being a stay-at-home mom isn't as easy as it sounds. Between cleaning up after everyone, checking homework, preparing lunches, catering to everyone's needs, I must also plan time for myself.

I was on the elliptical machine rocking out to an old Beyoncé album when I felt this guy eyeing me from the bench press station. His incline lifts didn't distract him from staring a hole into my head. I looked the other way initially, but when I looked back, I still hadn't lost his gaze. He smiled, and then winked. I rolled my eyes so that he would get the picture and continued my workout. At the gym, guys seem to stare or pass out lame lines like Jehovah's Witness pamphlets, so I'm used to it. Establish your boundaries early, or just ignore them altogether, and they usually leave you alone.

I guess I was a little curious, because I looked over to get another glimpse of him. Besides, he was some nice eye candy. By the time I glanced over, he was already gone. I thought, *where did he go so fast? Oh well.*

Suddenly, I heard a sensual voice behind me say, "Looking for someone?" It shocked me to the point that I almost fell from my machine. "My apologies. I didn't mean to scare you."

"You didn't."

"I think these are your keys. You left them on the Stairmaster."

"Thanks."

"I'm Dante."

At this point, I was no longer looking at his face. Brother was cute across the room, but up close he was fine! And I mean, *fine* fine. His arms were chiseled like a

Greek god, and his teeth were like perfect porcelain and extremely white next to his full lips and smooth, brown skin. His hands were huge, his nails were clean, and I could tell from his gym shorts that brother had it going on down there too. I thanked him for my keys and decided it was time for me to go, because a sister was getting heated and not from the workout.

That night, I followed my normal routine. I kissed the kids goodnight, wrapped my hair, kissed my husband before checking my alarm, and I dozed off. And then, I dreamt about Dante.

In the dream, we met in the gym just as we had that day, but this time, he was walking out of the steam room wearing nothing but a towel.

"You can't be on the gym floor in a towel," I told him.

"No problem." He dropped the towel immediately. He grabbed me, pick me up, and bent me over a machine. It was everything! I even had a shaking orgasm. The entire time, I could hear him calling me, "Baby. Baby! BABY!"

"Yes!" I woke up next to Jeff calling me.

"Baby, are you okay?"

"Yes. It was just a dream."

"What were you dreaming about?"

"Oh, nothing."

"Since you're up, how about I put you back to sleep?"

I smiled as Jeff climbed on top of me. He engaged in some good sex just as we always had, but that night it was extra good because I thought of Dante the entire time. What the hell was wrong with me? I didn't even know this guy's last name. Why was I obsessed with him? When Jeff finished, I rolled over, went to sleep, and secretly vowed to not think about Dante again during sex. I was a grown woman in a happy marriage. I needed to pull myself together.

The next day, I went to the gym. Sure, I was going for a workout, but deep down I hoped to see Dante. My gym sessions never usually ran over 45 minutes, but I stayed for 2 hours hoping he would show. After hours of jumping from one cardio machine to another, I left. This behavior continued for two weeks. He was never there. Perhaps that was a good thing. Why was I trying so hard to see this guy anyway?

I started to neglect some domestic duties by staying at the gym for so long. The house hadn't been cleaned, laundry had piled up, and I was in the streets looking for a man that wasn't even mine. The guilt set in, and I decided to head home.

As I was leaving, I saw him walk into the gym and my body froze. *What should I do? Do I speak? Will he speak? Do I play it cool?* In my mind, I was playing it cool, but my body was frozen in time. He saw me and walked over.

"Well look who it is—the lady who can't keep up with her keys."

I smiled and told him to shut up like a 16-year-old girl.

"Good workout?" he asked.

"Yeah, I was just heading out."

"Oh dang! I was looking forward to watching you run today."

"You creep," I flirted.

"No. I promise. You just have a nice stride."

"A nice stride, huh?"

"Yeah, amongst other things."

"Thank you."

"So, can I get your number?"

Fuck! It brought me back to reality when he asked for my number. I'm married with kids! Sure, I wanted to *look* at him, but I didn't plan to actually sleep with him or even get to know him. However, he wasn't deserving of a diss. *What should I say?*

"No, but I'll take yours."

"Mmm okay. So, you want to be in charge? Okay then."

I gave him my phone, and he entered his number and saved it under "Key Keeper." I walked out of the gym and sat in my car. It was almost scary how much of a hold that man had on me.

He was all I thought about at home that evening. I wanted to call so badly, but I couldn't. I had sex with Jeff that night, but I was fucking Dante in my mind. Jeff even commented that it was the best sex ever. What was going on with me? It was the second time I had fantasized about Dante while with my husband. It wasn't right, and I knew it.

A few days later, I stopped by the grocery store to fill the fridge for the week. With two growing boys and a husband, I couldn't keep anything in stock for too long. After the grocery store, I decided to stop by a local smoothie shop. I'd heard from others that it was good, but I hadn't had a chance to try it.

I walked in and heard a familiar voice, "Look who it is." It was Dante. Lord, this man looked even better in his day clothes.

"Are you stalking me?"

"Quite the opposite. You're at *my* job."

"You work here?"

"Most days. I own the place."

"Nice!"

"What can I get for you?"

"What do you recommend?"

"I recommend we lock the door and go in the back."

"Sir? Do you treat all your customers like this?"

"Only the ones who lose their keys at the gym."

It was merely flirty and cool until Dante walked from behind the counter and right up to me.

"I've been thinking about you," he whispered with heavy, intoxicating breath.

"You've crossed my mind." I initially held back. "Actually, I've been dreaming about you."

"I have that effect on people. I want you."

Who was I kidding? I wanted him too. A rush of emotions came over me; it was euphoric. I could not believe what came from my mouth next. "Lock the door."

He locked up the shop, and we went to the back. He gave me the best sex I've ever had in my life. Sex with Jeff was good, but Dante's was amazing. It could have been the excitement of it all, but I climaxed three times—twice in the back office, and then on the front counter. I'm quite certain a passing patron saw my ass, but I was so into it I didn't even care.

After we finished, he asked, "Now, can I have your number?"

That's when reality set in. I have a husband and two kids. What if it was Jeff who walked by and saw my ass in the air at the counter. I got dressed quickly.

He yelled as I walked out, "What? What did I do? Is everything okay?"

That night, I laid in bed next to Jeff and the guilt started to eat me alive. Jeff was a great man—an excellent man. Women would kill to have him. What had I done? Should I be honest and tell him? Come clean? Should I take it to the grave?

Weeks passed, and I had decided to keep my secret a secret. I stayed away from the gym and the smoothie shop. The guilt was extreme. I also didn't have sex with

Jeff for weeks, and I wondered if he started to suspect something.

I needed to clear my mind, so I decided to attend a yoga class at a spot near my house. There were a few ladies there, so I began to stretch before the instructor arrived. The instructor was none other than Dante himself. *What the hell!* Why was this man everywhere?

When I saw him, thoughts of getting my family and life together went out the window, and all I could think about was climbing back on his dick. I stayed for the yoga class and, fortunately, he didn't make it awkward. Yet, with every pose, I imagined him on top of me, under me, over me, inside me.

After class, the other ladies left, and I headed to the door. He stopped me and asked, "Are you just going to leave?" And less than 5 minutes later, I was ass-naked on my yoga mat doing downward-facing dog, cow pose and all the other poses I had just imagined with Dante.

What was it about him? Sure, he was fine, but I had seen fine men before. Hell, my husband is fine. I knew that if Jeff found out about us, it would be the end of our marriage as we knew it. I couldn't write off my actions as a mistake because it had already happened twice, and I couldn't promise there wouldn't be a third. This man put me in a trance every time I saw him. When I didn't see him, I was thinking about him, and losing my mind over a man whose last name I didn't even know.

It has been about two weeks since I last saw Dante, and I'm afraid of what will happen when I do. This is why I need therapy. It is hard to control myself. Jeff gives me stability like I deserve and he's the love of my life, but Dante gives me a high like no other. Jeff deserves an honest wife and someone who isn't boning Dante behind his back. Imagine if he found out. It would break him so bad, and I wouldn't have the words to take away his pain.

I know I would be pissed off if I learned that Jeff was lying in bed with me thinking about another woman, and here I am screwing another man. Am I now the woman black women hate? I have a good man at home, yet I'm out here screwing it up. I feel guilty. I feel dirty. I feel good. I feel bad. I'm all over the place. I need therapy.

Chapter Five Reflection

Have you ever encountered someone or something that made you do things out of your norm? What was it like?

_____

_____

_____

_____

_____

_____

_____

Is Girl 9 just excited about the thrill, or is she really over her current marriage? How would you proceed if you were in her situation?

_____

_____

_____

_____

_____

_____

_____

CHAPTER 6

GIRL 555: CODE SWITCHING

I'm not like most girls. I've been code switching my entire life. Most girls learn to code switch from their mothers. Think about it: when a bill collector calls, your mom says, "Hello, how can I help you?" When it's a homegirl on the other end, she says, "Chile, what's going on?" That's code switching at its finest, and we've learned to code switch in various areas of our lives—around white people, at work, or just among certain groups.

Basically, we have to turn it on. And I've been turning it on my entire life. Not just over the phone or at work, but in my own community. I didn't always look like the person I am today. I've gone through changes all my life and I'm almost ready to finally accept myself. My desire is to be comfortable staying there, and to heal old scars. I'm Girl 555, a woman of transition, and I need therapy.

I've always known I was different. When my mom would buy me toy soldiers and not the dolls I wanted, I would just pretend they were long-haired with rosy cheeks and high-pitch voices. After my dad would give me a haircut, I would tie a towel on my head and pretend to be a princess. When I had to look in the mirror and see outside pieces of me that didn't feel like they belonged, I would cry and imagine the day I could change the outside to match what was already inside me. I was different, but I grew up in a small town, so I had to play the role. Therefore, I learned to code switch at a very young age.

In grade school, other kids knew I was different. At recess, I would jump rope with the girls instead of dribble basketballs with the boys. The girls would ask, "Are you gay?" I would always tell them I wasn't, but I knew I liked boys. I could never bring myself to say it out loud.

Boys didn't pick on me too much at school. Perhaps they didn't know what to think of me. Plus, I had a best friend who was so loud and was always ready with the best jokes. And if anyone even shaped their lips to call me gay, she would go off. No one was exempt; she could send anyone home crying to their mamas. She was the only person I was comfortable enough to talk to about what I felt. When she had to move away because her dad had gotten a new job in the next town, she told me she loved me and to always be myself. We lost contact not long after that but, to this day, she was the only person who ever took up for me.

I tried to fit in. I tried to pray it away. I even tried to kill myself, because this world convinced me that people like me don't deserve to be happy and that's all I ever wanted. I just want to be happy. I didn't want someone's man. I didn't want to corrupt children—not that I could anyway. I just wanted to live my life peacefully. However, everyone and everything around me wanted to interrupt that peace. I can't even walk into a fucking restroom and sit down to pee without someone gawking.

I hear the bullshit from everyone—from all sides. The world's favorite line is, "I love you; I just hate your ways." That's bullshit. "I love you but not your ways" is a phrase Christians use to feel better about themselves and to justify their own sinful judgment. I AM my ways. It's inseparable. This is the way God made me. Why would someone *choose* to be ridiculed by society? Folks like that are why I stopped going to church.

Truth is, I grew up in church. My grandfather would preach every Sunday, and I would sing. He preached that homosexuality was a sin. At the time, I was almost certain I was gay, but Granddad didn't play that gay shit. As much as I did, there was no way I could come home and say I liked boys. I wasn't boy crazy by any means, and I wasn't driven by mere sexual desire. I felt trapped in a boy's body—one that wasn't my own.

While girls went to their moms for advice about their changing bodies, there was no one I could talk to about the changes I experienced and what I was going through. I felt alone. I was different, and no one wanted someone like me around. *Why would God make me like this? Why me? What did I do?*

It took me a long time to realize that nothing was wrong with me, and this is who I am. This is who God made. The government, the church, and most black people made me out to be a menace. They say I need to pray it away as if I haven't already tried—as if my parents and grandparents haven't already tried. Some others would say that it's just a phase—as if I would *choose* to be demonized by everyone on the street. They go as far as to say that I'm corrupting innocent children. I have never, and would never, touch a child—unlike the laundry list of priests accused over the past century who never get in trouble. I am simply a trans woman trying to be a good human.

You think I would choose this? You're right. Life is hard, so why would I make it harder by choosing to be something everyone hates? Believe me, if I could choose, I would be a straight man in a heartbeat, but I can't. If you think you got it hard, try being Black and trans. Try finding work when the person on your ID looks totally different from the one you're presenting to hiring managers. Try finding someone who accepts you for you. Try finding someone who doesn't just want to punch you in the face when you've done nothing at all.

You know, I've been beaten almost to the point of death. I first moved to the city after my parents put me out. All I had were the clothes on my back, a few dollars in my pocket, and the car where I would sleep. I pulled up to a gas station one night. It was late, and I hoped the darkness would conceal my features and allow me to pass as a woman. The dress I wore was all I had. Only the light of the moon could expose me, and I swore it wasn't bright enough.

Two guys stood outside the gas station. They watched me get out to pump my gas and began their catcalling. I knew they thought I was a cis woman, so I pretended I didn't hear them. I just needed enough gas to keep the car warm throughout the night. I was nearly finished when one of the men approached.

"I know you heard me calling you, lil mama. You can't speak?"

My voice wasn't very high, so I tried not to speak. I smiled and started to get back in the car.

"Nah, lil mama. You just gon' leave without giving me your number? Say something or I ain't letting you get back in this car."

"I'll take your number. Just let me get in my car," I said softly.

His smile turned to rage. All I wanted was to get in my car. I didn't call him over. I didn't ask anything of him but to be left alone, but he was mad.

He called his homeboy over, and I tried desperately to get in my car, but he punched me. They beat the dog shit out of me and left me bloodied at the pump. Cars came and went, but no one helped. Finally, a White woman drove up and called an ambulance. I went to the hospital beaten, bruised, and barely alive. The nurse wouldn't even touch me. I couldn't open my eyes because they were nearly swollen shut, but I heard her say, "He deserved this…walking around pretending to be a woman. He ain't a woman and it serves him right."

I just wanted gas for my car. When did that become a crime? Imagine if she was raped for getting gas, and someone said she deserved it because she was Black. Some people may never get it.

It was hard to survive the city on my own. I lived under a bridge for a while. Most times, I ate whatever I could find. I worked the corners. I've been raped so many times that it started to feel normal. The guys would pull up and tell me to get in the car. The irony is that it was always the hardcore, thuggish boys who wanted me. They wanted to see what was between my legs—touch it even. It turned them on. It was always the same. They would climb on top of me, do their business and, once they would cum inside of me, their eyes would turn. It was as if reality would set in, and they realized they had been pleasured by a transwoman. That reality caused them to hate me, but I believe they really hated themselves. They would tell me to take the money and get the fuck out of there. They would often spit on me or hit me before allowing me to leave. And of course, they would say, "If you tell anyone, I'll kill you." I knew it was a risk each time I slept with this type of guy. At any moment he could snap my neck for fear that I wouldn't keep his secret, and nothing would be done in my defense. Many of my trans sisters were killed in that way. What was the alternative? It was the only way that I could make money—the only way I could eat.

I reached out to people for help and always got the same answer. "No, we're sorry." I even went to churches, and they shut me out. I guess "come as you are" don't apply to people like me. And it's funny how preachers can encourage a liar, a drunk, or a backslider to come and be restored, but never seek out those in need of love to come and be loved.

I even checked myself into a mental institution because I figured with a life this hard, there must be something wrong with me. There was nothing wrong with me, but the institute pumped me with meds and gave me shock therapy for months. I'm surprised I still have the sense God gave me.

I eventually found refuge with my chosen family. It was a group of gay people who took me in as their own. They went to balls and competed for trophies like on that show, *Pose*. Most importantly, they loved each other, and they loved me. They provided food and shelter and told me that I was enough. I soon landed a job and was able to stop working the corners. I even went to community college and received a degree. I was able to save and get my own place. I would not be here today had I not found my chosen family.

Sometimes at night, I visit the corners I used to work and try to help the girls get off the streets. It gives me a sense of purpose—a sense of pride. Maybe God allowed me to go through so much pain to position me to help the next girl.

It took me a long time to stop feeling sorry for myself. Everyone's so fucking sorry for what I am and what I put my folks through. They can keep their *sorry*. I've gotten a lot of *sorrys*, but only one "I forgive you," and it's for myself. I forgive myself for not accepting who I was a long time ago. I am a woman of trans experience but, most importantly, I am a woman—a woman who needs therapy.

Chapter Six Reflection

Have you ever had to code switch? What was the experience like? Is it okay to code switch or is it a problem that we often overlooked?

_____

_____

_____

_____

_____

_____

_____

What has been your experience with trans people? If you believe in Black Lives Matter, are black trans people entitled to the same respect and response?

_____

_____

_____

_____

_____

_____

_____

CHAPTER 7

GIRL 40: PARTICULAR AGE

How did I get here? *How did I get here!* I guess I used to be an "it" girl or, some might say, a rather wild child. I partied hard throughout my 20s, 30s and 40s. I enjoyed life, enjoyed being a woman, and enjoyed being me. Now that I am a woman of a particular age, I look back and feel like I have more days behind me than I do ahead of me. Perhaps there is a lot more life to live, but I'm a little nervous about what the future holds. What's most apparent is that there is no one with whom I can share this next chapter of my life. You can call me Girl 40, and I need therapy.

I was an independent woman like most young ladies claim to be these days. I never wanted to get married. I made my own money, so there was no need for a man to provide for or protect me. Provision and protection came with a price I wasn't willing to pay. I could buy whatever and do whatever on my own, so I didn't need a husband or even a date. It didn't stop them from applying for a nonexistent position though. At bars, I hardly bought my own drink. Men would flock to my seat and bow at my feet, and I could have a different gentleman caller every day of the week.

It was flattering to have them press hard for my number or a chance to sleep with me. Hell, a few even proposed. And no, I wasn't sleeping with them all. I had a regular sex partner when I needed a piece, and he was solid, but oh, did they try. They would make bets to see who could get my number first. Sometimes, I would give my number to the lame guy of the group just to boost his confidence and leave the others puzzled and jealous. It was all fun and games.

I was the *it* girl, the bell of the ball, if you will. My girls Tonya, Tiffany, and I were the dynamic trio. We were like the Supremes. All of us were, as the young people would say, *hot girls*. Each of us came from small towns to begin college at Spelman and stayed on the same floor in the dorm. We had big dreams. Although we knew we would be successful in our fields, our biggest goal was to break as many hearts as we could.

None of us planned to get married. It was a game among friends. And note that was before cell phones, so we would give our dorm room's number to random guys and wait to see who would get a call first. We were thick as thieves. You didn't see one without the other on or off campus.

In my 20s, I went to the same nightclub every weekend. We would stay on the dance floor all night and dance to each song with a different guy. Every club owner wanted us at their club because we knew how to party, and the guys were ready to see us. Every sorority had approached us about attending an interest meeting, but we weren't interested. Our objective was to party and have a good time.

Graduation didn't change anything. We all received job offers in the city and purchased townhouses near each other. Boutiques loved to see us coming. Thursdays were specifically reserved for shopping for weekend party dresses. It is my belief that we kept the boutique on Auburn Avenue in business.

Our 30s didn't slow us down much. We went to bars instead of high-energy nightclubs. I wasn't dropping it low, but we were still backing it up. Whenever a new bar opened, without a doubt we were on the VIP list. We never had to wait in a line. We knew most owners and promoters from Buckhead to Greenbriar.

Once, we almost had a bouncer fired. A new bar had opened in Midtown, and we knew the owner who had a couple of other bars in town. We came to the grand opening, and there was a line outside. Of course, we walked up to the door and exclaimed we were VIPs, but the bouncer said we weren't on the list.

"I'm sure we are," I insisted.

"I don't see your name, so you can get in line or leave."

I called the owner right then and there. He came to the door with haste, pointed to the list and said, "Their names are right there." We were listed as "ATL Peaches." The owner was so upset with the bouncer for being rude to us that he told him to go stand by the bathroom line until he could learn how to address the bar's patrons. We had a time that night.

Once those 40s rolled in, we were still hanging in there, but then life really started happening. Life had been happening all along, but I guess I finally started to notice.

The girls and I would still go to bars, but Tonya got married. Just as I suspected, she lost some of her freedom. She didn't go out as much. When we would invite her, she would have to call for what seemed to be her husband's permission and make sure he didn't have anything planned. Then she became pregnant and was restricted to bed rest due to her age. After her son was born, her priorities changed, and it was almost impossible to connect with her. I wasn't jealous, but a little spiteful. We were living the dream, and she gave it up for a man. I loved and spoiled my godson though. He was so cute it, and he softened my heart to forgive her.

Tiffany's mother was aging and needed someone to take care of her. Because Tiffany didn't want to put her in a home, she knew she would have to move closer to her mother to become her primary caregiver. The company that employed her had open positions in her hometown, and she transferred to be closer to her mom. I understood why she left, but the selfish me didn't want her to leave. Even without my closest friends, I would go out from time to time because I could still have a good time by myself, but it wasn't the same.

One day, you're sitting at the bar and the men who once flocked to you and your girls are now groveling over the next girl. I understood; I wasn't 20 anymore. Old men at bars liked to look at young girls; the young men at bars were on a quest for a sugar mama, so they would wink and flirt with me. I must admit, I took some of them up on their offer a few times. If all they needed was a phone bill paid, I had it if I could get some young meat. However, young boys don't know what they're doing. They have the stamina, but no rhythm. They sure are nice to look at though.

I remember when I met JaQuan. He had more abs than I had patience enough to count, and even with his clothes on I could tell he had enough penis for 3 or 4 women at one time.

He approached with a pretty smile and said, "What's a lady like you doing in a bar like this?"

I smiled and said, "Enjoying a drink."

"Can I get you another?"

"How old are you?"

"I'm old enough."

"Mm hm… and I'm old enough to be your mother."

"I like older women. They know what they want."

"Is that right?"

"Yep. So, what do you want?"

"Right now, I'd like to go home and get out of these shoes. What do you want?

"I want to go home with you."

"Well, walk me to my car."

He walked me out, and I knew he was a broke college student, but I didn't care. He had chosen me.

Maybe it was a lie, and he just needed some money, but for whatever reason, he chose me.

Once we were at the house, I kept my hand on the pistol tucked into my purse just in case he was crazy, but he was actually nice. He told me to sit on the couch and he removed my shoes to rub my feet. He started to kiss my leg and work his way up between my thighs. He stood up and removed his clothes, and every inch of his penis was rock hard. I thought he might knock something out of place with it. He put on a condom and penetrated me. I was initially excited, but he didn't know what he was doing. I told him to stop.

"What's wrong?"

"I'm not a 20-year-old girl. I'm a grown woman. If you're gonna put all that in me, you gotta know how to use it."

"Well, teach me."

At first, I rolled my eyes. I'm too old to teach a man about sex. After I sat with the idea a little longer, I thought *why not*. He was my little project, and by our 3rd or 4th time together, he knew what he was doing. Chile, I didn't know I could still cum, but I taught that boy the motion of the ocean. His lil ass was obsessed with me too. Our fling lasted a few years. Sure, I paid several of his bills, but I didn't care. I had plenty of money, so why not?

After JaQuan graduated, he told me he was offered a job on the west coast. I was happy for him and insisted that he take it. He would visit from time to time, until the day he told me he had found a girlfriend and wanted to propose to her. I couldn't be mad. I was more than 30 years older than him and I'm sure he wanted a family and children. I couldn't give him that.

He came to Atlanta and said that he wanted to make love just one more time. He must have really had feelings for me. I put on something sexy, we did the do, and he spent the night. Over the course of our *situationship*, he had never spent the night. It was nice to have someone hold me. Although I knew it was just for one night, having someone breathe on me felt good.

The next morning, he rolled over and said, "I guess this is it."

"I guess so."

"I'll see you around. Maybe when I come back to town…"

"No, this is it," I said with much solace. I wasn't angry, but he was about to be a married man. I have always been a party girl, but I've never been a homewrecker.

I told him, "Goodbye. Go be the best husband to that girl, and don't you sleep with any other women, including me."

He looked at me and nodded his head before he walked out the front door. I watched as he got into his car and drove off. I knew I'd miss him, but it was time— past time actually.

When he was gone, I went to the bathroom and looked in the mirror. I really *looked* in the mirror and had a moment. You know, the moment when you suddenly realize your breasts don't sit as high as they used to, your skin isn't as tight as it once was, and the way you used to jump up in the morning...well, you just move a little slower. I walked into my bedroom and sat there. I waited for the phone to ring, but it never did. That's when I realized I was alone.

I found myself between a rock and a hard place—too old for a seat at the bar and too young for a granny wig and a house full of cats. I never had children, so there's no one to check on me. There is no man to accompany on trips to foreign places. When I called to check on Tiffany, she reminded me that a man wasn't needed for travel. And it's true. I don't. I've done numerous solo trips, but after a while, you want someone to share it with. Lunch at a café in Paris has a stench of loneliness you don't sense at the bar in Applebees.

I found myself lying awake at night wondering about the decisions I'd made. There are days I wonder about the road not taken. What if I had married and had kids? And then there are days when I wouldn't change a thing. If I could do it all over again, I don't know if I would change a thing. This may sound a little sad, but I've lived my life; and I've enjoyed every moment of it.

So, why do I need therapy? Maybe I don't. Maybe I just need to talk. Maybe I'm scared of the next chapter—afraid to end up in a home and with no one who cares enough to visit. Will I die alone in a room that smells like old people and Jello? Will no one remember the ATL Peaches and how we would cut up all over the city? Maybe I need some reassurance—someone to tell

me that the road not taken is as pretty as the one I've
traveled—and is also just as ugly. I need therapy.

Chapter Seven Reflection

Write about an experience or opportunity you didn't take. Do you regret it?

_____

_____

_____

_____

_____

_____

_____

_____

How often do you reflect on your life and the choices you've made? How do you feel about your decisions?

_____

_____

_____

_____

_____

_____

_____

_____

Do you fear that when you reach a particular age you will wonder about the road not taken? How could you avoid future regrets?

_____

_____

_____

CHAPTER 8
GIRL 911: POSTPARTUM

My number should be 911 mainly because I know I need help, and because 911 also saved my life. I've accepted that I need therapy, but I can't bring myself to say it out loud. I'm dealing with postpartum depression, and my fear is that by admitting I need therapy, I am also admitting that I am a bad mother. The realization may even mean I'm a bad wife and perhaps a bad person. I don't want to be a bad person. I need therapy.

"We're having a baby!" It's one of the most exciting announcements anyone could ever make. Personally, I could not wait to call my mom and share the news. People are usually pumped and excited about the announcement, the pregnancy, the gender reveal party, the baby shower, and then, before you know it, the baby is here. And nothing can prepare anyone for life after a new baby.

Mine wasn't the easiest delivery. I pushed for 5 hours, and she refused to come out. Soon, I became exhausted, and the machines started to beep. Fear set in. Was something wrong with the baby?

According to the doctor, I had stopped dilating and they would need to perform an emergency C-section. The horror stories that quickly came to mind made me nervous, but I wanted my baby to be safe, and I wanted to live to see her. After another hour, we had an 8-pound-11-ounce bundle of joy.

My mom made it just in time to greet her new grandbaby. Everyone was able to witness the process as they watched our social media to see what pictures we'd post next. When Ciera was born, the "congrats" flooded in along with the gifts from the people who forgot to send them beforehand. She received so many items that I would not have to shop for at least two years. Everyone was excited about Ciera, but no one checked on her mother.

People would ask how I was, and I'd respond, "All is well," which was enough for them to move on. All wasn't well. Recovering from the C-section was a painful process. It hurt to move. Furthermore, Ciera wouldn't latch on when I attempted to breastfeed. I felt inadequate—not even good enough for my baby to receive nourishment from my breasts. The shame of not being a good mother was almost instant, and I was quickly overwhelmed. I wasn't comfortable talking about it.

Although my mom didn't mention it, she must have sensed that something was wrong. She stayed with us for an additional two weeks to help with the new baby. The C-section caused me to walk around bent over like a little old lady. Some days, the pain was so unbearable that I couldn't hold Ciera. It was nice having my mom around because she was quite helpful. She cooked, cleaned, and took care of the baby while I rested and pumped. Before that, I didn't realize how much I would need my own mom as a new mom, but I was grateful to have her.

After a month, mom had to go back home. Fortunately, by that time, I could finally stand up straight and was doing much better. She even froze a few meals for me before she left. I wasn't ready for her to go, but I knew she had her own home and a husband who needed her as much as I did. Before leaving, she told me I would be okay and that she was just a phone call away.

I tried to convince myself that everything was fine, but when my mom left, I felt alone...and with a newborn. I thought I could lean on my husband, who was very supportive, but when his leave was over, I was alone again. Mom was gone, my husband was at work, and all my friends were quickly over the initial excitement of a newborn. I was alone.

The change I experienced was monumental. The lack of sleep and a baby crying through the night left me feeling depressed. My hair started to shed. My skin was dry. I didn't know what was going on. I considered that what I was experiencing was postpartum depression. I had heard a little about it but wasn't completely familiar. After reading a few blogs, I was convinced it wasn't my struggle. If it was postpartum, then I was surely a bad mother, and I wasn't willing to accept that. I had to be strong and get through it.

At my checkup, the doctor offered me pamphlets on postpartum. I said, "Thanks, but all is well." He must've known something was wrong because he shoved them into my hands despite my resistance. A few days later, I looked through some of the pamphlets, which were very different from the blogs. I even visited an accredited site for more information. And there was so much out there. Many seemed to struggle with postpartum depression. There were meetings and counseling sessions equipped to help sufferers. *Should I make an appointment?* Perhaps it was time to get help, but

I told myself I could get through it. It would be my secret. I knew I needed to talk to someone, but I didn't know who or how. I was ashamed.

I smiled through FaceTime calls when people wanted to see Ciera. They had no idea that I lacked the energy to shower most days. I became so good at hiding it that even my mom didn't notice. I mastered saying "All is well!" when it really wasn't. Things were horrible, but I kept pushing forward. I had to appear to be okay and that's just what I did.

It went on for months. I thought I would feel better. I thought if I pushed my way through, I would find my strength. Pretending became increasingly harder.

One day, my husband came home from work, and he must have realized that something was wrong. The woman in the living room chair was not the wife he once knew. I knew my face was fixed in a blank stare, but I couldn't resist it. Dinner had not been prepared, and I still wore my pajamas.

He asked, "Honey, are you okay?"

I knew it was my chance to say something. *Tell him you are not okay.* I opened my mouth to tell him the truth, but the words just didn't come out. Instead, I said, "All is well, honey."

He asked if I was sure, and offered me a second chance to come clean, but I refused to surrender to the truth of my affliction.

I said, "Yes. I was a little tired today, so I figured we could order pizza." He loves pizza so he thought nothing of it. I was dying inside and couldn't tell my husband. I cried myself to sleep that night, just as I had countless nights before.

I finally reached my breaking point, and the day came when I would end it all. I ran myself a bath and gathered leftover pain pills from the surgery. The plan was to overdose in the bathtub.

I placed Ciera on my breast to feed her for what I thought was the last time. I cried as I cradled her in my arms and told her how much I loved her, but that she would be better off without me. I began to reminisce. I'd had a great life, but I was convinced that the good days were already behind me. Life had become more than I could handle. It took Ciera longer than normal to fall asleep that day—as if she wanted me to hold on a little longer. I wasn't worth holding on to, and nothing in me felt worthy enough to hold on to her any longer either. I was damaged. When she finally fell asleep, I kissed her before placing her into the crib, and was sure my husband would be home by the time she awoke.

I grabbed my phone to leave my family a final goodbye. As I walked into the bathroom, the phone rang and the caller ID read "911." *Why would 911 be calling me?* It was awkward, so I answered.

"Hello?"

"Ma'am, this is 911. Someone just called and we were disconnected. I am calling back to make sure that you're okay."

"I'm sorry, but no one here called 911."

"Ma'am, my name is Ashley. If you're in any kind of trouble, it's okay to let me know."

"All is well." I really was good at saying it.

"If someone is trying to hurt you, ma'am, just say 'yes.'"

"No one is here except me and my baby."

"Awww, you have a newborn?"

"Yes, I do."

"I have a 6-month-old boy."

I wondered where she was going with the small talk. Plus, she was interrupting my plans. "That's good, but I really need to go."

"Okay. Make sure you sleep while your baby is sleeping,"

"That's what they say, but when else could I get anything done?"

"You can't do it all, ma'am. I had to learn to just do what I can."

"What do you mean?"

"You're just one person and you have to rest and take care of yourself."

"That's an understatement." I was over the call but still somewhat intrigued.

"Tell me about it. Three months ago, I found myself in a bad place, I was dealing with postpartum so badly that I contemplated suicide. I almost did it too."

"Really? What stopped you?"

"I looked into my baby's eyes. I started to put her to sleep, and she just wouldn't stop staring at me."

"It gave you the strength to go on?"

"It gave me the strength to accept that it was postpartum and that I needed help."

I held the phone in silence. I had just laid Ciera down, but I wanted to see her. When I walked into her room, she was wide awake in her crib. I looked into her big, bright eyes.

"Ma'am are you still there?"

"Yes, I'm here."

We continued to talk and even cried together. An hour passed and I was still on the phone with Ashley when my husband arrived. Before I knew it, I had a newfound will to live, and I finally had the strength to share with my husband what was going on. He was genuinely concerned and immediately took a few days from work to help me out and keep an eye on me. The doctor was able to provide the help I needed once I was honest. He prescribed a medication and recommended therapy.

After a few weeks, life improved tremendously. I had managed to climb completely out of the darkest season of my life, and I thought of Ashley and how she helped save my life. I wanted to thank her, so I talked to my husband, and we decided to call the 911 dispatchers for an address to send her a gift. However, I was informed that no one by her name worked there.

"There must be some mistake."

"An Ashley hasn't worked here in over five years," the supervisor said.

"Perhaps the young lady was using an alias."

I gave him the date and approximate time of the call to check his records, and he placed me on a brief hold. When he returned, he told me that there was no record of a call to my phone line. And it became clear that Ashley did not exist. She was my guardian angel, and she saved my life.

After weeks of medication and fully opening up to my husband, I am finally ready for therapy. It's still hard to say out loud, but I've learned to take it easier on myself. Postpartum may be over but we've considered having more children and I want to be prepared. I told myself that if I ever need help, I will say something, and I wouldn't let the condition linger. I am in control. It is also important that I stop living in denial when things are not good. It is impossible to hold *everything* together all the time. It is okay if everything is not well. I'm human, and we could all use some help sometimes. Right now, I need therapy.

Chapter Eight Reflection

Write about a time you were too prideful to ask for help.

_____

_____

_____

_____

_____

_____

_____

CHAPTER 9
GIRL 5851: VULNERABLE

I'm Girl 5851, and I need therapy. I chose that number because I have a problem with being vulnerable. Well, it's not so much about being vulnerable in general; I struggle with being vulnerable with men. I thrive on power and being in control. Once I show any sign of weakness, I will forever be under his authority.

I'm not mean. I'm not overly assertive. I can let him wear the pants in the relationship, and yet refuse to let my guard down and expose myself to him fully. That, I simply cannot do. It is easy to question whether he's the right man for me, but I assure you he is. He is amazing. It's me, and I don't want to lose him. Unfortunately, it may be too late. So, I'm in a place where I must admit that I need therapy.

John and I met 9 months ago. It was late—around 10 pm on a Friday. I was at a bar on the corner of 9th and West St. I liked to go there to clear my head and have a drink. It started to rain once I was inside the bar. I had just purchased a new pair of Louboutin's and didn't want to get them wet, so the moment could not easily be forgotten. I wore a brown trench coat, and my hair and makeup were done to perfection.

I had just ordered my second round when the bartender said, "This one is on the guy in the blue suit."

Though flattered, I wasn't impressed by a guy buying me a drink. Men bought me drinks all the time. It was rare for me to pay my own tab, and a sister can drink. When I looked over at him, he didn't look like the typical drink-sender. You know, the one who thinks that because he bought a $10 cocktail, I suddenly owe him some pussy. No, he was different.

I looked down the bar, made eye contact, and mouthed "thank you." Most men would see it as their window to come over and shoot their shot. Instead, he nodded, and mouthed "you're welcome," and continued to watch the game. This intrigued me. How dare he just send me a drink and not approach. I didn't like it. This isn't how it works. So, I decided to send him a drink. The bartender delivered it to him with a chuckle, and I waited for him to look over at me. This guy mouthed a petty ass "thank you" and continued to watch the game.

I figured he had to be gay, but the type of gay that can celebrate a bad bitch when he sees one, because let's be clear, I'm a baddie. It was possible that he wanted nothing more than to acknowledge me, but I had never bought a guy a drink without an *appropriate* response. *Am I losing it?* No way. I looked at my watch and noticed I had to get back to work soon. I was ready to drop it. Who cares about the guy in the blue suit.

I heard a thunderous yet passionate voice over my shoulder. "Thanks for the drink, but I'm more of a bourbon guy." What kind of charades was he playing?

"You're welcome," I said with a peculiar half smile. "Really into the game, huh?" I was confident this could be the only reason he hadn't approached sooner.

"Not really. Just passing time. You okay?"

"I'm good. Why do you ask?"

"You seem stressed."

"How so?"

"I don't know. I bought you a drink because you looked like you were worried. Maybe you were meeting someone who didn't show, or maybe you don't want to get those shoes wet in the rain."

Is this guy psychic? I know he can't read that on my face. I couldn't be truthful and let him know that his theory was absolutely correct. "No, I'm just having a drink before work."

"Nice. Well, see you around," he said as he exited the bar.

What the hell? He didn't even ask for my number. I said, "fuck it," tied my coat, and decided to head off to work.

Once I arrived at work and began to change out of my rain-soaked clothes, I couldn't help but think about the mysterious guy in the blue suit from the bar. Who was this guy? Why was I so wrapped up in him? I put it behind me as I headed to the floor.

I kept my eyes peeled for my next victim, and suddenly I heard that voice. "Fancy seeing you here." I knew exactly who it was—the guy in the blue suit. I turned to hide my excitement. He must have followed me. The ball was back in my court.

"So, you're stalking me now?"

"Not at all."

"How did you know I was here?"

"You said you were headed to work, and this is the closest strip club to the bar. I just took a chance."

"Sure."

"It's true."

"Well, Mr. Blue Suit, as you said, I'm at work. So, if you want to talk, you have to get a dance."

"How about we go to the VIP suite?"

"It's $300. You okay with that?"

"I think I can manage."

I escorted him to the back room—still intrigued. It was nice to dance for someone I found attractive. I told him to have a seat. I stood in front of him and began to unbutton my blouse, but he stopped me.

"Slow down. Why don't you have a seat?"

"Look, it's gonna be $300 whether I'm clothed or naked. Totally up to you."

He pulled out $2,000 and said, "Here's $300 for the dance, and the rest for those shoes you were so worried about."

"How did you know that?"

"I pay attention."

"Sure. So, what do you want from me?"

"Why do I have to want something from you?"

"You just gave me $2,000, and you don't even know my name. You want something. We *are* in a strip club, so I assume you want some pussy."

"I'm not an ugly guy. I can get pussy. I just want to talk for now."

It was slow. There was no way that I would have come close to earning two stacks that night without Mr. Blue Suit's kindness. We talked the rest of the night and laughed at the silliest things. I hadn't loosened up with a guy in that way for so long. Hell, I couldn't remember the last time I actually *liked* a guy. I keep my guard up. As a dancer, I must. I can show no signs of weakness. If guys see us as weak, they take advantage. If another dancer smells weakness, some poor girl is definitely getting robbed.

In that moment, however, I let my guard down. I was light, and no longer carried the weight of the world on my shoulders. And I sensed that if I did, he would bear the burden with me.

Before I knew it, the lights were up, and it was closing time. I had spent the entire night with this man in the VIP room—fully dressed. I craved more of this happy place that I never knew existed until now, but there was something about the lights coming up that wouldn't let me. I bore my soul to him, and he knew things about me that no one else knew. *How could I be so vulnerable?*

I didn't know this man, and I was being stupid. He had gotten in my head. For sure, it was a ploy to get in my pants, and I had fallen for it. *How could I be so dumb?*

I could hear my mom's voice in the back of my mind, "This is a man's world. They all want something from you, and once they get it, they don't want you no more. A woman has got to be tough—especially a Black woman. Don't show no love."

"I have to go," I said to John.

"May I give you a ride home?"

"No, I'm good."

"May I have your number?"

That's what I wanted to hear. I was back in charge. "No, but I'll take yours."

I got his number and waited at least two weeks before calling him. I typically don't call the men whose numbers I collect on the job, but I couldn't get him out of my head. I had never felt the way he made me feel that night. My guard had been burned to the damn ground, and I'd gotten a taste of what it means to be vulnerable. It felt good, but could I trust it? Was it a set-up to be hurt?

I can't be a trusting girl. It's weak and pathetic. Why would I give others a shot to take advantage of me? I decided to call him, maybe even enjoy his company, but I would not let my guard down under any circumstances. I had this on lock. *Clink, clink!* I would not be the weak dancer who is rescued by some tall, handsome man. I'm my own woman and will always be.

I called John, and we went out. He was a gentleman with a bit of an edgy side, and I had a great time. We went on a few dates over the course of nine months. We would visit new and creative places, and I would always drive myself. If I went back to his place, it was only because *I* wanted to go.

One night, we sat on the roof of his high rise and watched the sun go down. Afterwards, we made love on the roof under the stars, and it was *everything*. There was something about the stars mixed with the thrill and fear of getting caught that made it explosively erotic. He thought for sure I would stay the night that night, but I couldn't. If I stayed over after sex, he would think he was in control, and I couldn't let that happen.

Two weeks ago, we went on a date. We were at the end of dinner when he asked me what was wrong. I told him that everything was fine because I was really having a good time.

"I truly enjoy your company, but ever since we met, you've seemed guarded."

"I'm just protecting myself."

"From who? Me?"

"Maybe."

"You don't have to protect yourself from me. Let me be your protector."

At that moment, I realized why I was so guarded. No man had *ever* been my protector. My father wasn't around in my youth, and I've always protected myself from bullshit. I knew that if I was going to be in a serious relationship, I would have to be vulnerable, and I simply wasn't ready for that.

"You want to be *my* protector? You met me at a strip club and now you want to wife me?"

"I met you at a bar actually. And why don't we start with girlfriend?"

"And you don't have an issue with me dancing?"

"Not if it's what you want to do."

"What man wants his girl to be a stripper?"

"I didn't say I *want* you to be a stripper, but I know who I met when I met you. Do you dance because you don't want anyone to get close?"

"No. I dance because it pays my bills."

"Interesting."

"What is?"

"You will bear your entire body in front of a group of strangers, but you won't bear your heart for one—me."

"I can easily put my clothes back on, but once I expose my heart, it'll only hurt me in the end."

"Not with me."

"Of course not. I have to go." I got up to leave.

"I want to be with you, and I'm willing to give you time, but I won't stand on the outside of your heart forever."

"Good night, John." I walked out, got into my car, and headed home.

John was right, but I would never admit it. Why was I like this? I refused to let him in completely, and I wanted to—damn near needed to—but I couldn't.

John called the next day, but I didn't answer. I didn't know what to say. I avoided his calls and texts for a few days. The truth was that I missed his company. I wanted him around, but I wanted it on my terms. I wanted to be vulnerable with him, but something inside me would not let me.

After two weeks, I decided to call him back. I could tell he was upset, but it was obvious that he still cared about me. I couldn't fix my lips to say, "I was sorry," so I offered to take him out instead.

He asked to meet at the bar on 9th and West where we first met, and I agreed. When I hung up the phone, I dolled myself up to the gods. If I wasn't ready to let him in completely, I had to keep his attention in other ways. I went to the back of my closet and pulled out Lulu— my weapon of choice. Lulu is the dress that hits every curve just right. Once he saw me in Lulu, I knew he would look past my faults.

When I walked into the bar, I first noticed John, and he looked as handsome as ever. His eyes caught a glimpse of Lulu and I swear I could see his dick jump through his pants. Lulu works every time.

I walked over with a sexy stride and knew with certainty that there would be no talk of letting guards down that night. All that'll be on his mind was getting my panties down.

"You look amazing," John said with a twinkle in his eye.

"Thank you. You look good as well."

"How have you been?"

"I've been good. How are you?"

"I'm well. Missed you these past 2 weeks."

"I missed you too, but let's not talk about that."

"I think we should."

"Maybe we shouldn't. I look good. You look good. Let's just move forward."

"I really want to do that, because you're looking fine as hell in that dress, and I want nothing more than to take you home and rip it off of you."

"Then let's do that."

"I can't. I care about more than your body. We've been doing this tango for nine months, and I don't want to waste anymore of our time. The first night we met was amazing. You laughed and talked, and I believed you were someone I could be with for a very long time— even the rest of my life. I haven't seen *that* girl since. You are so guarded. I've been patient, and I really want this to work, but I can't keep hoping it will get better without seeing any progress. You need therapy."

"I need what?"

"Therapy. I know we as Black people don't talk about it much, but you do. And that's not a bad thing."

I lost it. Who the hell did he think he was to tell me that I needed therapy?

"John, how dare you tell me that I need therapy. Yo' busted ass needs therapy."

"Don't get defensive. I've been to therapy. I was a lot like you. That's why I approached you nine months ago."

"You didn't approach me. You bought me a weak ass drink."

"I can see this is going the wrong way."

"Damn right it is."

"I think I should go."

"I think that's a good idea."

Before I knew it, I had thrown a drink in his face. I was furious. He had the audacity to tell me that I needed therapy. Who the hell was he to tell me what *I* needed?

Once I gathered my thoughts and walked out of the bar embarrassed by my actions, I got home and looked around. I had a spacious penthouse with nice furniture and a spectacular view, but I didn't have a single friend to call and explain what had happened. There were a few girls from work that I talked to, but just like I struggled to let John in, I never really let them in either. Hell, I don't think I ever mentioned John to anyone. In my entire adult life, I had never gotten close to anyone. I have vulnerability issues. John was right. I do need therapy.

Chapter Nine Reflection

Girl 5851 uses Lulu to deflect from her lack of vulnerability. Have you ever tried to distract someone who cares about you from seeing your issues? How did that turn out?

_____

_____

_____

_____

_____

_____

_____

_____

What are Girl 5851's strengths and weaknesses?

_____

_____

_____

_____

_____

_____

_____

_____

GIRL 444: SAVED

I'll go by Lady 444 as this number represents love and wholeness. It represents a deep love for something or someone. Personally, I love the Lord. He alone has gotten me through so many trials and tribulations that I don't believe I need therapy. I was taught to take all things to the Lord in prayer, and to let *Him* be my counselor. I'm only here because, if I'm honest, I haven't gotten over *it*. For that alone, I might need therapy.

There's not much to tell. You see, I've gone to church since I was a wee little girl. I sang in the choir and was a junior usher. Actually, I did it all. Pastor Brown would preach, "Hold on to God's unchanging hand." Oh, I would praise Him from the rising of the sun to the setting of the same. My God! Yes. We would make a joyful noise until the power of the Lord came down.

I was a wholesome girl all through high school, and afterwards I took up a few classes at the community college. However, I remained faithful to my church and became leader to First Lady's armor bearers. I didn't date much in college because men had other things on their minds, and I was looking for a God-fearing man. I wasn't in a hurry, so I waited patiently for the Lord to send me a husband.

I met my Malcolm for the first time at Mt. Moriah Baptist Church. We both attended a pastor appreciation program that day, and when he went into the pulpit to read the scripture, Sister Morton said, "That's your husband."

"What?"

She repeated, "That's your husband."

His brows were tense, and he didn't smile. I could tell he had nice teeth only when he opened his mouth to read. I could find no softness in him, but he was indeed a tall glass of water.

"I don't know. He looks so serious," I told her.

"He *is* serious…about the word of God. He's clearly a man of God if he's been following my husband for as long as he has."

"Is he…experienced?"

She laughed. "About as much as you are."

I smiled, and then I looked to Malcolm and wondered if he had noticed me too. To my surprise, he walked right up to me after service.

"Good evening, ma'am."

"Good evening." I couldn't help but blush a little.

"I don't want to be out of order, but I had to come and speak."

"Well, I appreciate it, and I'm glad you did."

"I'd like to take you to dinner if that's okay with you."

He was a gentleman, and I could tell he was nervous, but I obliged.

We courted for a few months. The entire congregation seemed happy for us. We went on many dates to get to know each other and to just spend time in each other's company—but mostly in the daytime. To tell the truth, our urges were getting the best of us, but I remained a pure, woman of God. Yes, our spirit was strong, but our flesh was weak. So, we told Pastor we wanted to get married, and a few weeks later, we were.

I loved my Malcolm. He was the best husband a woman could ever want. He worked hard, was a God-fearing provider, and a true head of the household. He treated me like his queen, and I had no reservations about submitting to him. That man was deserving of more than I could ever give him. He was everything I asked God for in a man—even physically. He was tall and chocolate. Plenty of sisters wanted to get their teeth into my Malcolm, but he was a good man—a faithful man.

The happiest day of our lives was when I came home to tell Malcolm I was pregnant. If it was a boy, I wanted him to be Malcom Jr., but my husband didn't agree.

"No, let's name him Josiah after my grandfather, Joseph," he said.

He wanted his son to carry on the legacy, but still have his own identity. I thought it was absolutely wonderful.

My pregnancy moved so swiftly. The church honored me with a baby shower, and through their prayers, Josiah was spiritually covered and blessed well before he took his first breath.

The day Josiah was born was a day I'll never forget. It was an easy birth, and after just a few pushes our pride and joy was here. He loved me so much. We were a happy family that placed our faith above all things and God at the center.

Josiah proved himself smart and talented throughout the years. We were proud of him, and he loved us so much. We could almost count on him to make us laugh, and Malcolm and I had never experienced anything more fruitful than parenting our precious boy. As Josiah grew older, he and his dad became closer and closer and were together all the time. Josiah participated in numerous high school sports and earned himself a scholarship. When he went off to college, we lost him.

One day, Josiah came home for a visit, or so we thought he did. He pulled up in the car we bought him, but something else got out—something ungodly. He walked into the house where he was raised, which hadn't changed a speck, but the house itself wouldn't recognize the young man that entered it.

"Mom, Dad, this is who I am now."

Malcolm thought it was a joke. He said, "Boy take them clothes off."

Josiah said, "This is how I dress now, and I'm gay."

"Say what now?" Malcolm was puzzled.

"Dad, I know it may be hard to understand, but if you'll just let me explain..."

Malcolm had already heard enough. He couldn't bear to look at his son in leggings and a tube top. He said to him, "Take those clothes off right now and act like a man."

"I am a man—the man you raised me to be, honest and truthful. This is my truth."

"I ain't told you to be no sissy. Now take those clothes off, or you can get out of our house."

Josiah refused and begged his dad to hear him out. They argued for a while before Malcolm slapped Josiah to the ground.

Josiah, young and strong, had the ability to really hurt Malcolm if he so desired, but he didn't. He would never disrespect his father—even after his father struck him down. Josiah got up from the floor and looked at me with a gaze I've never seen before. His eyes, which I thought would be filled with hate and rage, were glossed over like a 5-year-old boy. He looked to his father for acceptance that he knew would never come. As glossy as his eyes were, not a single tear fell from them. Josiah just turned and walked away. He got into the car and took off down the road. I never saw him again.

The moment was paralyzing. When I think back on it, I realize I just stood there. The whole time they were arguing, I just stood there. I never opened my mouth. And when he left, I stood there some more. I couldn't move. Many thoughts flooded my head. How could he do that to us? How could *my son* do that? That wasn't my child. I didn't raise him like that—to live a sinful life. I'd rather my son be in jail or *dead* than to be gay.

Malcolm and I were never the same after that. We were convinced that we'd failed as parents. No pain in this world compares to that of losing a child. We went to God and told Him we'd do anything if he'd just give us our son back—*anything*. And still, nothing. It was as if God had shut us out. We prayed and prayed and even went to our pastor, but he advised us to let it go. I had served in that church my entire life and all he could say was "move on" when I lost one of the most important people in my life. I swear I tried, but Malcom just couldn't. It ate away at him, and his prayers didn't seem to work. He went to Josiah's campus and tried to reconcile with him, but it didn't work. He fasted for days. And when that didn't work, he believed that God had forsaken him. He fell into a deep depression soon after and Malcolm was no longer Malcolm. His worry and broken heart ushered him right onto his deathbed, and my Malcolm had left me too.

Most days, I don't want to get out of bed. I never cease to ask for the Lord's help, and He's helping me each day. Nothing has filled the void of missing Malcolm and Josiah. When people ask Josiah's whereabouts, I simply say, "We lost him, and he's not coming back."

I couldn't face another situation like the one I faced with Quincy, my brother. He was a few years older than me, and he was my best friend. When we were young, you couldn't see Quincy without seeing me. Quincy was always the life of the party—always smiling and joking. Actually, Josiah reminded me so much of him. The ladies loved him. He was handsome and well put-together, but Quincy had a soft side.

He and his friend, Kevin, would go on a fishing trip every few months. We knew Quincy couldn't catch a fish to save his life, and that it was a lie, but it was 1983. Mama didn't say anything, because back in those days, if you didn't say anything, it didn't happen. He'd go on those trips, stay a few days, and come back home to us in one piece. Wasn't no need questioning him if everything was alright.

Except one time, he didn't come back for a week. Mama sent our cousin, Jody, looking for him. Jody was the cousin we called to take care of things—and by any means. Jody came home and said he found some of Quincy's clothes, and the cabin where they stayed looked as if it had been robbed. He said there was blood everywhere, but he couldn't find Quincy. Mama told him to go back and to not return until he brought her baby home with him.

As Jody walked out the front door, a White man approached. The man told us that he had Quincy's body in the trunk. Mama asked what happened to him, and we were told that he fell into the river and a few *real* fishermen found him floating there. Mama knew it was a lie, but what could she do? As a resident of a small, Alabama town in 1983, when a White man brings your son home dead, you tell him, "Thank you," and send him on his way.

Quincy's body was beaten so badly that we could hardly tell it was him, but the heart-shaped birthmark on his right arm was undeniable. We buried him and, to keep the family name out the mud, we told the town he had drowned—but we knew. White men found Quincy and Kevin up at that creek and tortured them to death. As a child, his death traumatized me. What made it worse is that I couldn't talk about it to anyone. My brother was killed for his lifestyle, and no one paid for it. There's not even a mumble about him anymore. And I still miss him.

So, to me, Josiah is gone. I lost my boy. I can't go through it again. What they did to Quincy was unimaginable, and I can't bear to have it happen to my son. The world is mean—even more mean for people like that. So, I told myself I lost my child long ago. I lost him in his sleep. He went peacefully, and now he's with his father.

The lie I consistently tell myself is starting to lose its power, and I can't help but to miss my son. I don't know where he is—if he's alive or dead. I don't know if he misses me or even cares. What I *do* know is that I miss my son, my husband, and my brother. The Lord keeps me daily, but I need some help. I guess I do need therapy.

Chapter Ten Reflection

What do you have in common with Lady 444?

_____

_____

_____

_____

_____

_____

_____

What emotion is 444 really dealing with and not admitting to? Have you ever had an underlying emotion that you masked with another emotion?

_____

_____

_____

_____

_____

_____

_____

CHAPTER 11
GIRL 333: ANGRY

Call me Girl 333. It means ambitious, driven, successful, and focused. I have always been the head of the class. In high school, I was voted most likely to succeed. I was both president of my class *and* homecoming queen. I had beauty and brains and was determined to be a CEO in corporate America.

I married my college sweetheart, and he played in the NFL for a few years, but I was still determined to finish school and begin my own career. Unfortunately, it wasn't as easy as I thought it would be. I was always tenacious, but I was also humble, considerate, and kind. Life, however, has a way of turning you. I never wanted to be an angry Black woman, but here we are, and now I need therapy.

As a strong, Black woman, I learned to command any room I entered early in life. It was not about my voice but my presence. My presence said *I am here, and I know what I'm doing* without me ever opening my mouth. It said that I was intelligent and highly capable. Despite my intelligence, my beauty and race would often throw off the others in the room. They couldn't fathom how a Black woman could be so bright as well as attractive. It was hard for my White counterparts to understand that a middle-aged, Black woman knew more than a young, White guy fresh out of college.

It was easy for me to understand since I had worked extremely hard for everything I had. I studied in college. I graduated with a double bachelors in Economics and Finance, and all while I worked a part-time job. The young, White boys were only hired because *Daddy* knew someone. They weren't well-versed on their roles and lacked experience but somehow felt they should be the boss. They were the absolute worst. I tried not to let it get to me, because at the end of the day I knew I was the best at my job, and no one could do it better than me. I didn't need work friends. For as long as I was paid on time, I would endure the racism, sexism, and nepotism.

I earned a position at DNC Productions years ago as the team lead of a production line, which was a promotion from a previous company. As I think back, I don't know if DNC *wanted* to hire me or if they were merely meeting their affirmative action quota. I quickly learned the ropes at DNC because I knew that if I didn't produce, I would be left out to dry.

We had bi-weekly leaders' meetings, and the goal was for each of us to produce at 90%. From my perspective, and with my experience, this bar was incredibly low, and I knew I would exceed the expectation. There were seven leaders. Five of us reported between 89-92%. A White guy, who was the champion of the company, and who just so happened to be the boss's nephew, reported 98%. Everyone clapped for him and gave him an *atta boy*. They told him his skills must be genetic because he really knew what he was doing.

When my report proved that my team was performing at 103% eyes began to roll. When the White men looked over at me, it didn't read, "Wow, she's doing a great job," but rather, "She must be fluffing her numbers." Not a single leader inquired about my strategy—at least not in front of the others. It was only *after* the meeting that I received calls to meet up with them and share some tips. They wanted to know how to do it, but they wouldn't dare give me any praise or ask for help in front of our colleagues. My confidence enabled me to share, but I knew to never give away *all* my success secrets, and especially not to those who wouldn't have my back and were possibly hoping for me to fail.

Over time, they began to treat me like I was one of the boys. I even developed a relationship with another team lead. We went out for drinks a few times after work, and I once shared my ideas to grow the company. Unfortunately, I had become too comfortable.

One day, in our monthly strategy meeting, the big boss requested growth strategies for the upcoming quarter. My coworker, with whom I'd shared my ideas, was eager to answer. He stood and courageously shared my ideas as if they were his own. He never acknowledged that it was my idea or that we had spoken about it. The room applauded him and offered an abundance of kudos. If looks could kill, he would've died that day because my eyes cut him deep. I couldn't believe it. I trusted him.

The idea was later implemented, and he was offered a promotion shortly thereafter. That was my promotion, and he knew it. I called him to my office and told him I didn't feel it was fair and that I deserved to be acknowledged for my input. He claimed it wasn't my idea and that we were just bouncing ideas off each other. He said if I felt so strongly about it, I should go to the big boss. He knew I couldn't go do that. As the only female—let me rephrase—the only Black female at that level in the company, I would only look like a complaining, angry Black woman. So, I had to let it go, but inside, my meekness was turning to anger. It was the biggest lesson on never telling them all my secrets.

The idea I had was great, and while he figured out how to implement it, he had no idea how to sustain it. Of course, he wanted me to partner with him under the guise of possibly getting a promotion myself. I declined to work with him and said I would take a backseat and see where he ended up. Ultimately, it didn't go well for him, and the company was suffering. There was nothing he could do.

Meeting after meeting, the big bosses became increasingly agitated with the plan, and right when the project looked like it would destroy us completely, I jumped in and saved the day. With ease, I provided the missing pieces to the sustainability plan, which I never shared with him. It was all we needed to turn things right-side-up again. I'd had them the whole time. So, in front of the corporate bosses, I showed them what I was working with, and they finally noticed the jewel they had in me. By the following week, your girl was promoted, and I left the boys in the dust. I continued to grow in the company over the years, and I thought it was where I would have even more longevity.

While in a meeting one day, they announced that we would get a new partner, and that we would start to report to the new partner the following week.

Someone asked, "Who is he?"

The gentleman from HR said, "You mean *she*."

I was so excited that it was a woman. It would be nice to see another woman in a position of power. She would possibly be someone I could relate to and share my ideas.

They gave us her name, so I decided to put Google to work and find out more about her. When her picture popped up on the screen, and I noticed that she was also a Black woman, my excitement grew. Things were about to be on and poppin'. There would finally be someone who could understand me, someone I could talk to, someone I could trust, someone who could help balance the bitterness I felt because of the boys and tip the scales back over into kindness.

When she began as the new partner the following week, I couldn't wait to introduce myself. After the introduction meeting, I waited while everyone else threw their pitches at her. I walked into her office with a big smile on my face, and she barely lifted her head from her desk to acknowledge me. I went on to say how grand it was to see an African American female in her position, and that it was an honor to work alongside her, which got her attention. She looked up right away, but not with excitement in her eyes like I'd imagined; it was a look of disgust. Her expression made it clear that she was not about helping other Black women get to the top. She was there and wanted to be the only one. What I thought would be an encouraging moment in my life turned out to be one of the worst experiences I've ever had.

She said, "I'm your boss and I'd appreciate a little notice before you barge into my office."

"Yes, ma'am."

"And for the record, I realize we share skin tone, but you *will* respect my position and I expect your work to be exceptional."

"Yes, ma'am."

I thought to myself *maybe she was just being hard on me because she wants me to be successful.* I get that. Black women must work exceptionally hard to compete, and she wasn't going to do me any favors. I was okay with that because I didn't need favors. I was intelligent enough to stand on my own.

When we began to have regular meetings where we reported our performances, she was just like the White men before her. I was a top performer and she never recognized it. Again, I was overlooked. It was almost as if she wanted me to fail. She would give me extra assignments and tight deadlines for completion. I endured her wrath for months, and then one day she called me into her office.

I figured the hazing was finally over and she would let her guard down, say that I passed the test and that I endured well. I was wrong. The heifer fired me. After all the hard work and long hours I'd dedicated to the company, she fired me. She said the company was downsizing and was forced to let some people go. I lost it. I went completely off and showed my ass. To this day, I'm ashamed of the words I used. Security was even called to carry me out.

I was disappointed in myself, but I was even more disappointed in her. She was a Black woman, and she fired another Black woman without proper cause. How could she do this? I wasn't incompetent. I was one of the best employees there. The incident proved that some women simply cannot handle competition.

I left determined and headed straight to a competitor's company. My goal was to never stop until I drove them out of business. However, after I acted a fool when I was fired, I was blackballed in the industry. I was deemed an angry, Black woman, and I couldn't land an opportunity anywhere in my field. I would have to start over, but I'd worked too hard to be in such a position.

Years of hard work had been wasted. Sure, I hold myself accountable for acting crazy when I was fired, but it was what she wanted all along—to destroy me so that she could be the only one. Thankfully, my husband and I were financially secure, but I found myself hating her. I wanted to harm her. You have no idea how much I've seen her car blow up in my mind's eye.

I was nearly over my fury until I flipped through *Black Enterprise* last week, and there she was—the sole Black female CEO. I was so mad. She wanted to be the only one. Why did it have to be this way? As a Black woman, she had oppressed her own people. I wanted to get back in the game, but years had gone by. I was out of touch, but I wanted her stopped, and I found myself stalking her online. I was once a nice, driven woman. Now, I'm just angry—an angry, Black woman, and I need therapy.

Chapter Eleven Reflection

Have you ever been called an *angry, Black woman*? Were you actually angry? How did it make you feel?

_____

_____

_____

_____

_____

_____

_____

Have you ever been misunderstood and resorted to anger?

_____

_____

_____

_____

_____

_____

_____

How do you manage a situation where you thought someone would have your back and they didn't?

_____

_____

_____

_____

_____

CHAPTER 12
GIRL 7: WHOLE WOMAN

Well, I'm Girl 7. I chose 7 because the bible says that 7 represents completion, and I am a complete woman. I have accomplished a college degree, a faithful husband, and three beautiful children. I am the complete woman. I have everything I need, and everything I've ever wanted. I've heard the age old saying that women can't have it all. Typically, a successful career and a great husband and children don't mix. When I was a little girl, I said I would defy the odds and have it all. I would be the first Black, female CEO of a company. Now, I'm a grown woman, and some would say I have it all. The only thing I need now is therapy.

I used to have dreams. I didn't have small dreams either. They were big. I wanted it all—a top career, to sing in a band on the weekends, and a family. I wanted everything, and I felt like I could have everything. I went to college on a music scholarship. Music was always a passion of mine. I never wanted to be Beyoncé, but I craved being in musical atmospheres. I double majored in Music and Marketing, so it was perfect when I landed a job at Arista Records. I led their marketing team three days a week and was a top performer. I specialized in results.

Let me tell you, the guys at my job couldn't handle me. They knew I could get the job done, and I took my job very seriously. However, I always made time for myself. My girls and I used to hang out all the time. Every Thursday night was girls' night. We would go to the bar and cut up. On Friday nights, I sang with a local band, so people knew me, and it was always a good time. Guys would come in and try to talk to my girls and I, and we would always pay them dust. They'd get no attention. I was living the life. The only thing missing was a husband.

When I met John, we didn't hit it off immediately. I'll never forget how I walked into my office one day and the guy was just there.

"Umm. What are you doing?"

"Oh, you must be the cleaning lady. We want to get rid of all this stuff."

"Excuse me?"

"Yeah. I assume the last person didn't clean their office. I can help you, but all of this must go."

"Sir, I don't know who you are, but I'm *not* the cleaning lady."

"Oh, I'm sorry. I just assumed… I'm John Carmichael."

"Nice to meet you, John. Now, tell me what you're doing in my office."

"*Your* office? I'm pretty sure this is *my* office."

"And I'm pretty sure I'm not being fired, so this is definitely my office. Who are you?"

"I'm the new consulting attorney, and they told me I could have office 506."

"Got it. Most attorneys pay attention to details."

"Yes, most do. I'm exceptional, so I always do."

"So, tell me, John, how did you miss that *8* on the door? This is office 508. Not 506."

"Dang, I feel like a fool."

"As you should."

"So, what do you do here?"

"I'm head of marketing."

"Wow. Well, if you'll let me take my foot out of my mouth for calling the head of marketing the cleaning lady, I'd like to apologize."

"It's fine, John. It's nice to meet you. Are you from here?"

"No, I just relocated from Dallas. Do you think you could show me around?"

Was he flirting with me? And after he just called me the cleaning lady? Oh, the audacity! He was handsome, but I wasn't going to let him off that easy.

"I'm busy, but perhaps the cleaning lady can show you around," I taunted.

"Ouch. I'll see myself out."

When he got to the door, he looked back and smiled as if to say, "Yeah, I'm gonna pull that."

The following Friday, I was performing with the band, and in walks John. He looked nice in a suit, but in regular clothes the brother was fine. I never noticed people from the stage, but I noticed him. After my set, he walked over to me.

"Well, if it isn't the head of marketing. It looks like the company should be marketing *you*."

"No, I sing for fun. I never wanted to be a star— just sing on occasion and be the head of my department. I see you found your way around the city."

"Yeah, I asked the cleaning lady. Turns out she was booked too, so I'm just winging it."

"Poor guy."

"I know, right? But it looks like I found the right spot."

"Looks like it."

"So, what are you doing after your set?"

"I'm going home."

"Would you diss me if I asked you out for a cup of coffee afterwards?"

"For a cup of coffee, yes. For a round of drinks, I'd consider."

"Drinks it is."

I finished my set, and we went to an after-hours spot not far from the bar. It was cool. We drank and we danced for a while. He had rhythm, and I can't lie, I was smitten. He was the final piece to my puzzle. He was a successful guy, and he had the potential to be my husband.

We dated for a few months, and he really was the *right* guy. He proposed a few months later, and we were married soon thereafter. He bought our home in Sunny Acres, which has 5 bedrooms, a pool, and it's better than anything I could have ever imagined. I ensured that his suits looked nice, and that the house was properly cleaned. I know these tasks seem beneath a woman of my caliber, but it was imperative that I play my part. Perfection comes at an expense, and I paid my dues well.

Fast forward 10 years, and we now have three beautiful children. Keith plays basketball, so I take him to practice. By the time I get him there, it's time to take Denise to piano lessons. She finishes just in time to pick up Justin from karate. My kids are heavily involved and cultured and are such good kids. I cook dinner for them *every* night, and on weekends, we have family outings or mini trips, and spend summers at the beach.

You may think, "But you haven't said anything about *you*." Well, that *is* me. I'm the perfect wife and the perfect mother. I try to be, anyway. My family *is* my job.

Once the kids were born, it became hard to balance the marketing role, singing on the weekends, and going out with my girls. First, I let go of the band. I would still do a few corporate gigs, but every week was just too tough. Second to go were the weekly Thursday-night outings with the girls. We started to connect every other week, then every month, and now it's just whenever we find time. Before long, Thursday nights became phone calls, and then weekly texts. We now hear from each other every now and then. I held tightly to my marketing position, but at some point, John's career surpassed mine. He was making more money, and he also needed me more. If *he* didn't need me, one of the kids needed me. And then I became pregnant with Justin. I was so disconnected from work that the company started to suffer. John just always needed me and distracted me from what needed to be done at work. So, before they could get rid of me, I decided to resign.

My days are now consumed with taking care of the kids. I'm always in a carpool lane. If I'm not doing something for the kids, I'm doing something for John. If I'm not doing something for John, I'm cooking, cleaning, or folding clothes. Lord, there are always so many clothes!

This was the life I wanted. I wanted the husband and the kids, but now that I have them, I don't know who I am anymore. I went to the annual awards program at John's company, and he received the "Top Attorney in the City" award. Everyone cheered for him. He was so proud of himself. I was proud of him too, but a piece of me missed that. I wasn't jealous, but it caused me to think of my own dream. Was I really living it? I wanted to be the first, Black woman CEO of my company but, instead, I was just a housewife. It was cool, but it wasn't what I wanted.

That night, John was so happy. Since I knew it was a big deal for him, I tried to hide the disappointment I felt in myself. I was conflicted. We had great sex, which didn't take long because he was drunk, and then we went to bed. It seems that as soon as he climaxed, he was out, so I eased out of bed and went into my walk-in closet. I found an old box of awards and photos from when I first started at Arista. I thought, *look at me. That was someone I was proud of. That was someone others looked up to and aspired to be.*

I look at myself now, and where there once was a driven, independent woman, there is now someone's wife, someone's mom, someone's cook, someone's maid. I see the lady John *thought* I was when we first met in my office. What happened to me? Like really…what happened to me?

I decided I wanted to get back out there, so I applied for some marketing jobs. I had been out of the workforce for so long that I would have to start from the bottom and work my way back up. I considered starting my own marketing firm, but who was I kidding? Where would I find the time? After talking to John about it, he simply said that I didn't need a job, and suggested that we take a vacation instead.

We travelled out of town and stayed for a week. Ultimately, it did nothing to fill the void. I didn't need a getaway, I needed to find me. I considered joining the band again, and actually did for a few weeks. When you have small kids and a husband who travels for work, you find that band life just isn't for a middle-aged mother. I had to let it go.

Everything that defined me so many years ago were gone. The kitchen, a cleaning rag, and diaper changes are what presently shape my identity.

Where is the lady with the corner office at Arista Records and why can't I seem to find her? It's not just about a job. Where is her drive? What is her identity? I would have been open to at least meet the wives of my husband's coworkers, or the parents of my children's friends, but my entire life now revolves completely around my family.

I love my husband and my kids. I do. Sometimes I find myself sitting quietly in my living room but screaming inside. No one hears me. I am merely a fixture, a do-girl, Mrs. Hold It All Together.

They say women can have it all, but can they? If so, how can they do it and maintain their sanity? I love my family and wouldn't trade them for the world, but I need help to find who I am again. I fear the day I regret the decision I made to be a full-time mom when my kids are grown and gone. What if John leaves one day? I don't think he will, but what if he did? Who would I be then? My entire existence revolves around John and the kids. I must find myself, but how? How do I balance the kids, my husband, cooking, cleaning, and being at everyone's beck and call? I just want to get back to me. I promise I will do the work, but where do I begin? I need therapy.

Chapter Twelve Reflection

Have you ever lost yourself? How did you find yourself again?

_____

_____

_____

_____

_____

_____

_____

What must a woman do to have it all (a husband, kids, career, etc.)?

_____

_____

_____

_____

_____

_____

_____

CHAPTER 13
GIRL 0: BROWN SKIN

Brown skin girl. Skin just like pearls. I'll never trade you for anybody else!

I love Beyoncé for this song, but unfortunately, I was traded for everybody else. I heard brown skin, dark skin, black skin, tar baby, and blackie, but I was never called beautiful or cute. With a beautiful, light-skinned mother and three adorable, light-skinned sisters, I was the only dark child. I've learned to cope, but I don't know if I'll ever move past the traumatic experience of being a dark-skinned child in a society saturated with colorism. The number I feel most is 0. Zero: nothing, never enough, and having no value.

I was the knee baby with two older sisters and a baby sister. My mother was one-fourth Puerto Rican, but she grew up in a Black home. She was gorgeous with long, milky, black hair, thick thighs, and a shape that was out of this world. My father was handsome as well—tall with full lips, and super white teeth that beamed off his midnight black skin. Though dark, his skin was flawless, and all the women thought my daddy was a tall drink of water, but my mother was his pride and joy. My sisters took their light complexions from my mother, but I was definitely my father's child.

We all had the same features, and looked a lot alike, but because my skin was darker than my sisters', I was always side-eyed. I could hear the whispers. Does she have a different daddy? Who does she look like? Why is she so dark? My sisters were the recipients of compliments and praise and, to be fair, they *were* beautiful. My compliments were few and far between, but always carried a stipulation. I would hear, "You're cute for a dark-skinned girl," or "You have some pretty skin." I could never just be pretty. I tried to ignore it, but it surrounded me.

When it was time for school dances, my sisters were always asked out by the guys on campus, but I never was. For one school dance, we all went to the mall to shop for dresses, and a local designer approached my sister.

"Excuse me. Do you model?" she asked.

"No," my sister said.

"I would like for you to model some of my designs. How old are you? Are your parents around?"

My mom overheard the conversation and was skeptical but flattered. Once she realized the lady was legit, my mom said that she had three other daughters who would be great also. The designer looked over and smiled. When she saw my sisters, her eyes lit up, but when she looked my way, the glow faded. It was clear that she only wanted my sisters.

"I believe I only need three."

"I have four daughters, so if you can't use four girls, we will pass," my mom said with a stern look, knowing exactly which daughter the designer didn't want. She was my defender and refused to subject me to petty discrimination. The designer allowed me to take part in the fashion show, but it was obvious she didn't want me there.

To her credit, my mother always validated me. She did her best to make me feel beautiful, but when everyone tells you that you aren't, it can be hard to believe your own mother.

My Aunt Renee, who's just as beautiful as my mom, babysat me and my sisters one day. While we played outside it the blazing sun, Aunt Renee said, "Okay, y'all come on in the house. I don't want y'all to get dark."

My sister said, "Just 5 more minutes?"

"Do you want to be as black as your sister? Get in this house! Your sister can stay out if she wants."

All the kids went inside except for me, and I was out there alone. For a while, I would call "green light!" and run until I called "red light!" to pause for a breath. If color could change course in such a way, my experience would be different. My life wasn't a game. Aunt Renee didn't make me stay outside that day, but her words made me feel like I was better off there. What was worse is that she didn't once yell for me to come inside. She didn't care, and none of my sisters came back for me. Perhaps they didn't do it to be mean, but when you're fair-skinned, you may not notice the oppression of a dark-skinned sister. I didn't hold it against them, and never brought it to their attention. I believe they would have stood up for me, but I didn't want to be the source of conflict. I was already dark, and that was enough of a burden on them.

On a separate occasion, when my cousin birthed a beautiful baby girl, my aunt, Carmen, came into the room. She took one look at the baby, and said, "Oh, good! She's light-skinned. Keep her greased up. I don't want her to lose her color."

I wondered what was so bad about losing her color. Was being dark that big of a deal? Would she not love the baby the same? I went home that night and talked to my mom. She always knew how to make me feel like nothing in the world mattered. She sat on the edge of her vanity and rolled her hair, and I admired how each strand was flawlessly tucked and secured. She would look in the mirror and hum as she combed and rolled, knowing it would fall perfectly the next day. She was beautiful, and I wondered how she could create something as dark as me.

"What's up, baby girl? Come sit by me."

I walked over and grabbed the makeup powder from the vanity. "If I put this on, would I be as pretty as you?"

She said, "No, baby. You are already prettier than me."

I began to cry. I wasn't pretty, and she knew it. I knew it. I couldn't form the words to express what I felt in that moment. It wasn't my intent to cry; the tears formed quickly and fell uncontrollably.

"What's wrong?"

"Am I ugly?"

She immediately stopped her rolling, and said, "No! Why would you say something like that?"

"Because my skin is dark. It's not like yours or my sisters'. My nose is long and thin, my lips are big, and I'm skinny," I responded.

Mom turned from her vanity and pulled me in for a big hug. She looked me straight in the eye. "You, my dear, are a special child. You are the most beautiful of all your sisters."

I looked at Mom as if to say, "Yeah right! Just tell me lies."

She said softly, "It's true. You are most beautiful because you look like me *and* have your father's color. I love your father's color. That's why I married him. You are dark, and people may treat you differently, but don't ever be made to feel like you're less than because of your skin. You are perfect. Perfect because you are mine and God made you. One day people will pay money to have lips like yours and people are already paying for noses like yours. And you just wait until your shape fills out, men will line up to take you on a date."

Mom's words made it a little easier to dry my tears, and I so badly wanted to believe them, but deep inside the damage was already done. She could tell that my insecurity hadn't lifted, so she sat me on her lap, and we played in her makeup.

She applied lipstick and eyeshadow, and said, "See, you are even more beautiful. You just wait, you'll be the belle of the ball in just a few years. Now, go get some sleep."

Mom was somewhat right. By the time I went to college, I had filled out. I was 5'9 with a shape like my mom's and had hair flowing down my back. Guys liked me, and that was something I'd never experienced before—being wanted.

There was one guy who was everything. He was tall and brown-skinned with enough abs for an entire NFL team to borrow a pack and still have some left. The day he walked up to me, I was in the student union. He asked me out and we dated for months. I really thought he could be my husband. We had sex a few times, and with protection of course, but one night everything changed.

We saw a movie at the theater and then went back to my place. While we discussed the movie in bed, he said, "You know I love you."

"You just tryna get some."

"No, I'm serious. I can't imagine life without you."

He pulled me in close and held me. We laid there for about an hour just listening to each other's heartbeats. He started to take off my clothes and then kissed every inch of my body. When he made it between my legs, I was already cumming, but he kept going. He put on a condom, and we made love like never before. I could feel every inch of him inside of me. I could feel every vein of his dick when he would thrust against my pelvic walls. We climaxed together and he just laid there inside of me.

After about ten minutes, which felt more like two hours, he got up to go clean himself off. Suddenly, I heard, "Shit! Fuck! Dammit!"

"What is it?"

"The condom broke," he said.

"Oh hell."

"Right."

"Are you on the pill?"

"Yea, I am. We should be good."

"I hope so."

"Me too. I'm not ready for kids."

"Right, especially not with you."

I paused. I knew that neither of us were ready for kids, but his statement made me realize that it wasn't that he didn't want them at that time, he didn't want them with me.

"Excuse me?" I probed.

"Nothing."

"No, what did you mean by 'not with you'?"

"Just drop it."

"No. I'd like to hear what you meant."

"Baby, can you let it go? It's nothing."

"No. It's something. So, tell me. Do you not want a dark baby? Am I only good enough to fuck?"

"Baby, you know how people are. I love you and I love your skin, but I don't want my child to have to grow up with people calling them blackie. Look, I'm considered brown-skinned, and you're darker than me. I just think…"

"Get out. Get out!"

I didn't want to hear the rest. The man I loved, and who had just given me the best sex of my life, ruined the moment because he nutted in me and thought I would produce a dark-skinned baby. He had been *my* everything for months, but as I reflected, things came into better perspective. He hadn't introduced me to his friends or family, and we always went on dates out of town or in an area far from campus. Was he ashamed of me the whole time? I didn't even want to know.

That was ten years ago. Since then, the natural wave came in, and with that, came "loving the skin I'm in" campaigns. I've learned to cope with my complexion. One method is to date White and Hispanic men. They often better appreciate my beauty than the brothers. To them, I'm exotic—a masterful creation. It's funny when Blacks know that I date outside my race and ask, "Why?" Women would rally behind Black men, and others would add their two cents about how I'm tainting our melanin. They emphasize how much they love melanin to make a point. I don't respond because all I can think is, "You love *your shade* of melanin. If you were my complexion, you wouldn't be so in love."

I haven't had any children, because I am too afraid. What if I have a little dark-skinned girl? Of course, I would validate her as often as I possibly can, but would I be okay if she shared my past experiences? Do I want her to suffer? I want a child, but it's almost evil to knowingly put another human being through what I've endured. I need therapy.

Chapter Thirteen Reflection

Write about a time when, consciously or unconsciously, you treated someone differently because of how they look?

_____

_____

_____

_____

_____

_____

_____

CHAPTER 14
GIRL 4: BABY MAMA

I wanna start with yo mama; she shoulda whipped yo ass. Know you aint shit, but she don't care 'cause you lit.

Summer Walker sang the hell out that line! I wish I had heard it five years ago. I need therapy. Bad! Before I met Tyre, I was a good girl. Well, I'm still a good girl, but now I have irreversible regrets. Maybe *regret* is the wrong word. We have a baby together, and I don't regret that part at all, but if I could do it all over again, I would. You can call me Girl 4 because I'm his 4th baby mama.

I met Tyre 6 years ago while hanging out with my girls. He walked over and was looking fresh, but I knew he was not the type to take home to meet mama. He was the type to take home for a good time. He was 6'2" with milk chocolate skin and a full beard that would make patchy men just cut theirs off and give up. He wasn't very muscular but had a nice body.

I promised God that I wouldn't have any more one-night stands, so when Tyre came over, I opted for a date night instead of some quick dick. So, when he asked if he could take me home, and flashed that bottom grill, I replied, "You sure can...after you take me to dinner, and we get to know one another."

I could tell that he was used to getting what he wanted, but not giving in to him immediately, drew him in even more.

He smiled and said, "That's wassup."

Tyre didn't have it all together. He bounced between jobs but always managed to keep at least one. He would spend nights equally between his mama's house and his own spot. He was charming, but in a hood kind of way, and always nice.

About six months into our relationship, he told me he wanted me to meet someone. I thought it would be his mother, but it was his son. I didn't even know he had a child, and we had been together for more than enough time for him to divulge this little tidbit. I found out later that Tyre didn't plan to introduce us that day either but was stuck "babysitting" the boy while his mother was away. Nevertheless, it was a conversation starter.

We went to the park, and it felt like we were a family. When I asked why he had never told me he had a kid, his response was, "I don't have *a* kid, I have two."

At that, I should've walked away. It had been six months and this nigga had never even mentioned a kid. I continued to probe and asked why he never brought the kids around, and he told me that baby mama #1 lived out of town, so he doesn't get to see them too often; and baby mama #2 was crazy, so he doesn't talk to her much. I didn't know how to respond. I despise men who trash talk their baby mamas, but I wasn't there and didn't know the situation. Hell, I had just discovered they even existed.

I must say, Tyre was a great father that day. His son looked at him as a prince would a king. I thought to myself, *maybe one day we could have a family*. I was fine with being a stepparent for as long as there wasn't any drama.

A month later, I found out I was pregnant. It wasn't planned, but we had unprotected sex all the time, so we knew it was a possibility. In a perfect world, I would be married first, but I have a career, and a family support system. Besides, Tyre and I had been together for seven months. We were on the same page, and he practically lived at my house. When he came in that day, I decided I would tell him over dinner. My assumption that he would be excited turned out to be so wrong. He was not.

"What do you mean you're pregnant? I already got two kids. What am I going to do with another?"

I burst into tears. He immediately ran over to comfort me and apologize. He said he didn't mean any harm; he just wasn't expecting the news. He said he was excited to have a baby with me because he knew that I was his rib, and that gave me comfort. Maybe everything would be okay after all.

My friends were geared up to spoil my baby and so was I. The pregnancy had to be perfect, so I signed up for Lamaze classes and everything. My first doctor's appointment was so special—for me. Tyre missed it, and said he was called in to work. I didn't sweat it. When he missed the gender reveal party, he claimed he was working overtime to get ready for the baby. And since there were mostly girls there, I didn't trip. However, when I got home that night, I walked in on him with another woman. They weren't in bed, but they sat together on the couch. I was heated!

"You said you had to work. Who is this and why is she sitting on my couch?"

"Baby, let me explain," he said.

"Someone better. Who the fuck are you?"

The woman said, "I think I should let y'all talk."

"No! You're in my house. Who the hell are you?"

She grabbed her purse to leave, and as she stood, I noticed she was pregnant.

"I think y'all should talk."

He told her, "No. Stay. We all need to talk."

"What is going on?" I asked.

"Baby, she's pregnant."

"Okay. Is this a sister I don't know about?"

"No, she's my baby mama—#3."

Before I knew it, I lunged at Tyre, pregnant and all. I wanted him to feel the hurt I felt. How could he! My emotions and hormones were all over the place and this only added to my troubles. To discover that he'd gotten another bitch pregnant on the day of our gender reveal, was stressful, so he took me to the hospital to make sure the baby was okay. The baby was fine, but Tyre's face was not. The doctor gave him stitches where I'd nearly clawed the lying bastard out of him, and I didn't care. It would be nothing compared to the stitches my heart would need.

To make matters worse, his mom showed up at the hospital with his other two kids and had the nerve to confront me about assaulting her child.

"Your son did this, and you ain't said shit to him about having a baby on me." Afterwards, I told that heifer to get the hell out and not to worry about ever seeing this grandchild.

Baby mama #3 was a *random*—a mere hole he crawled into and came out with more than he expected. I can't say that I was surprised. He claimed he slept with her only once, but we know that's a cheating man's go-to confession. He would still call me his queen, but that was indeed a lie. After that, he was always gone, and I spent the rest of my pregnancy alone.

After the third girl delivered their baby, I saw pictures on social media of Tyre holding him. His caption said that the baby was going to be a king and would never want for anything because "Daddy got you." Meanwhile, that nigga didn't even have a job. He was stuntin' and had people in the comments believing he was a great dad.

An entire three months later, I heard from his tired ass. He called and said he wanted to see me. I knew it would be some bull, but I told him he could come over. He pulled up in a new car, which I later discovered belonged to baby mama #3. Despite my amazement, he looked nice.

"Can we talk?" he asked.

"I'm listening."

"I owe you an apology."

"For?"

"I did you wrong. I can admit that."

"You did."

"I want to make this right. I want to be in my child's life."

"I won't deny you the right to be in your child's life."

"I also want to be in your life."

"Well, you're my baby's father, so we're connected for at least 18 years."

"I want to be more than just connected."

"I think we've passed that phase."

"Look. I know I messed up, and I get it, but I would like a chance to make this right with you. Remember when we first met? You are as beautiful today as you were then."

"Thank you, but beauty won't rekindle our relationship."

"I get that. I'm gonna keep trying though."

"You don't have to. How about we just co-parent?"

"I can do that."

"Thank you. I have one more Lamaze class if you would like to go." I didn't have much hope, but I'd be lying to myself if I pretended I didn't want to have a relationship with my baby's father.

"When is the class?"

"Tomorrow."

"I'll be there. How about I pick you up?"

I agreed, and when the following day came, I was slightly excited about going to class. Class began at 7 PM. When I hadn't heard from him at 6, I called. I didn't get an answer, so I decided to text to see if he was still coming. He responded that he was on the way. I smiled because I initially feared he would stand me up. However, after waiting for him past 7:30, I knew he wasn't coming.

A few days later, Tyre called my phone, but I didn't answer. A few hours later, he showed up at my house. Through the door, I asked what he wanted. He wanted me to let him inside, and I wasn't afraid of him, so I did. Tyre made the excuse that something had come up the day of the class, and he couldn't make it. I didn't care. I was over it.

"I have a very important question for you," he said.

"What is so important that you couldn't just text me?"

He parted his lips to ask, "Are you going to put me on child support?"

"Why?"

"Because I don't think you should. I'm going to take care of my baby, so we don't need the government telling you how much I'm supposed to give my child."

"The government doesn't tell you how much to give your child. Besides, you can always give more and do more."

"Yeah, but I don't like that."

"No, you don't like to be obligated."

"Nah, I'm just sayin'..."

"Please leave, Tyre."

Tyre was full of shit, and I didn't want to hear another word. I was done with him, and angry with myself for allowing Tyre to play such a big role in my life. I decided that this was my baby. I made my bed and had to lie in it.

When my water broke, I didn't call him. Maybe I was being spiteful, but I didn't care because I was hurt. He didn't see the baby for the first month. Whenever I would tell him to come over, he always had an excuse, or would say that he was coming and never did. It could only lead to disappointment when my baby was older, so I decided to never tell my child if his father was coming over. If he showed, he showed. If he didn't, he didn't.

Now, I'm a stereotype—a Black woman raising a son alone. Sure, he has uncles and a granddad, but his dad isn't around. I don't want to spoil him, nor do I want to be too hard on him. His dad still pops up every now and then, and I hear he's on baby #7 now. The problem is that I don't know what to do with a teenage son, and I don't know how to form a new, romantic relationship with him on my plate. I need my life back. I need therapy.

Chapter Fourteen Reflection

How do you manage regret?

_____

_____

_____

_____

_____

_____

_____

CHAPTER 15
GIRL 3659: ABUSE

No, no, no! Please don't! Not again! I used these words way too often, but this time was different. I meant it. I was not going to let him hit me again. After finally realizing my value, I was ready to fight back. It had to end, one way or another.

It is said that 3659 is a reminder to break free of confusion and uncertainty. However, that is exactly what I feel—caught between a rock and a hard place. Who am I kidding? It's not a rock and a hard place; it's a rock and solid ground. I can't seem to leave the rock for solid ground, which is peace of mind. What I'm trying to say is I need therapy.

Jeremy was the love of my life. We met in college and fell in love. He was everything that I ever wanted in a man. He was Black, educated, handsome, and always good to me—until he wasn't. The day we met, I was a college freshman and I lived in Denton Hall, which was right on the edge of campus. Freshmen had to walk what seemed like forever to get to class. He was a freshman also, but he was a local who lived off campus and had a nice car.

It was raining as I made my way to College Algebra, and he pulled up beside me. He asked if I needed a ride, and since I was getting soaked, I so badly wanted to get in. However, I didn't know this guy.

"No, thanks."

"Come on. It's raining."

The cars behind him were piling up and blowing.

He said, "Okay fine, don't get in," and zoomed off.

I felt like an idiot as I walked in the rain without an umbrella. He hadn't actually zoomed off as I suspected. He parked in a nearby lot and walked back to me with an umbrella, which was the sweetest thing anyone had ever done for me. He didn't know me, but said he'd passed me every day but never had the nerve to say anything.

We walked until we reached where his car was parked, and I accepted the ride. After that, we were inseparable. We dated the rest of the semester, and at the end of my freshman year we moved in together. My friends loved him. They knew we would be together forever. The only friend that wasn't a fan was Jennifer. Jennifer thought we were moving too fast and needed to slow down. Jeremy despised Jennifer.

Everything was perfect. We rolled onto campus together daily, would meet for lunch dates, and had study sessions in the library. He would even pick me up from work before heading home. Many nights, I fell asleep in his arms on the couch, studying or just watching TV. We spent every moment together, and it was heaven to me. After a while, I stopped spending time with friends. *Is this what he wanted?* We both graduated with bachelor's degrees, and he proposed on our graduation night. Of course, I said *yes*; he was everything I wanted in a man.

We both found amazing jobs and went on with life. Our days were mostly consumed with work, and we would spend the rest just enjoying each other.

After work one day, Jennifer called to ask me to go to dinner with her. She had not seen me since graduation, and really wanted to hang and catch up. I told her that I'd love to and that I really missed her. She was my best friend, and I hadn't seen her in years.

I scurried home and jumped in the shower without a second thought. As I stepped out of the shower, Jeremy arrived home. It was out of the norm for me, so he asked why I took a shower so quickly after work.

"You'll never believe who I talked to today."

He looked unamused.

I said, "Jennifer called, and she wants to go to dinner. I'm so excited! I haven't talked to her in years."

He looked at me with fire in his eyes. I had never seen it before. "You didn't ask me," he said.

"I'm sorry, babe. I guess I got so excited that I didn't even think about it. Do you want to go?"

"No."

"Oh, okay. Did we already have plans for tonight?"

"We don't, but you don't either. You will not be going out with Jennifer. Period."

I was confused. I remembered that he and Jennifer weren't the best of friends, but that never posed a serious issue before. I laughed it off.

"Jeremy, what are you talking about?"

"I said what I said. You're not going out tonight." The tone of his voice was weirdly intimidating, and one that I had never heard before. I laughed it off again.

"Move back so I can get dressed."

He grabbed my arm and threw me across the bed. Jeremy had never put his hands on me before. I didn't know what had come over him.

"Stop, Jeremy! What are you doing?" but he didn't stop.

That evening, I stood staring at a busted lip and bruises in the mirror and had no choice but to call Jennifer and say that I had come down with a stomach virus and wouldn't make it to dinner. She insisted on coming by to check on me, but I insisted that I was okay and needed rest because I felt weak, and even promised that Jeremy would keep an eye on me. That was the start of many lies to come. I honestly don't know why I lied. I was in such disbelief that Jeremy had hit me, anything was liable to come out my mouth. I loved him, and he loved me. He had never been aggressive toward me. What had come over him?

I never wore a lot of makeup, so imagine the looks I received from my co-workers when I walked into work the next day with my beat face. "I'm trying something new," I said. They loved it so no one questioned it; they just talked about how pretty I looked. I didn't feel pretty. Many thoughts raced through my mind that day. How could he do this to me? What had I done to make him so angry? Was he stressed? Was something going on at work? What could it be? Did he hate Jennifer *that* much? That was the beginning of a long list of excuses I'd use after he'd hit me.

That afternoon, I arrived home tired from work. More than anything, I was drained from thinking about the bruises beneath the makeup. I walked in to the aroma of dinner being cooked in the kitchen, and Jeremey met me at the door. It was strange because Jeremy never cooked. He came over and embraced me. Usually, I loved being held in his arms, but after the events of the previous night, it brought me no comfort.

He apologized repeatedly and said that he didn't know what had come over him. According to him, he was frustrated with work and had taken it out on me. He begged for my forgiveness, and I told him that it was okay as long as it never happened again. Of course, he promised it wouldn't. He said dinner would soon be ready and that he would run a bath for me afterwards so I could relax. I felt better. I know there's never an excuse to hit the woman you love, but everyone is entitled to making a mistake. We're all human, so I decided to let it go.

After dinner, Jennifer called to check on me. We talked while I soaked in the tub, and I let her know that I was feeling better, and we'd have to get together soon. Jeremy walked in and asked who was on the phone. When I told him it was Jennifer, he walked out, and I kept talking. As I prepared to hang up the phone, he came back in and dragged me out of the tub by my hair. He punched me in the back of my head so hard that I passed out.

I awoke on the bedroom floor the following morning and had to call off work. The first time may have been a mistake, but the second was not. The Jeremy I knew and fell in love with was no longer there. Perhaps that's what made me stay. Perhaps I longed for the love of the man I met on a rainy day in college. I knew he lived inside of this empty shell that was hitting me, and I so desperately wanted him to return. For whatever reason, he was gone. I should have left as well, but something wouldn't let me. I couldn't leave, and the abuse continued for years to come.

I often told Jeremy that we needed help. I asked him to go to counseling with me, but he refused. He said he didn't want people in our business, but I was tired of living a lie. I went to a therapist myself a few times, but unsure of how it worked, I feared the therapist might call the police, so I stopped.

Every day with Jeremy wasn't bad. When times were good, they were *really* good. It was as if there was a demon inside him that would suddenly come out, and I couldn't understand what triggered it. And no matter how poorly he treated me, I still believed he loved me. I spent so much time wondering how I could love him. Why couldn't I just leave? Why didn't I fight back?

When I found out that I was pregnant, I couldn't wait to get home and tell Jeremy. I thought it would make him happy, quench the rage within him, and bring the abuse to an end. When I shared the news, he was so happy. College Jeremy was back, and he was happy. That night, I thanked God as I figured the abuse was over.

One Saturday morning, at three months pregnant, I was lying on the couch when he rushed into the room. I knew something was wrong. He told me to grab a beer for him out of the fridge. I had been managing morning sickness all day, so I guess I wasn't moving fast enough. When I handed him the beer, he called me a lazy bitch, and I began to cry. It was probably the pregnancy hormones, but he didn't care.

"I'll give you something to cry about," he said. And he did. I ended up in the ER with a broken rib and three fractures. There was no more baby. I made up my mind at the hospital that I had had enough. It was one thing for him to hit me, but he had killed my unborn child.

The day I came home from the hospital, Jeremy was making breakfast in the kitchen. I walked into the kitchen and was not feeling my best. I had just lost my first child. However, he was excited about making breakfast for me. When I told him I wasn't hungry, he insisted that I sit down and eat.

"No, I'm good," I said.

He walked over and grabbed me. Normally, I would have fallen due to his strength, but not that day. Something arose in me that I had never felt before. I looked at him and screamed, "No! Not today!"

As his hand went up, I grabbed the knife from the counter. Before I knew it, I had stabbed him. If only I had gotten help before it came to that. If only I had listened to Jennifer. If only I had left him.

Jeremy died that night, and I've spent the last three years in prison. Since I had never shared the truth about the abuse or showed anyone my scars, no one knew. The judge didn't believe me. He lessened my sentence due to temporary insanity since I had recently lost a baby, but he gave me 10 years in prison. The prison sentence was nothing compared to the abuse Jeremy put me through on the outside. I allowed this man to ruin my entire life. I can never get back those years. I can never kiss my precious baby. I am up for parole soon, and I hope I can still have a normal life. The first thing I'll need is a counselor, because Lord knows I need therapy.

Chapter Fifteen Reflection

Is love truly blind? How often do we overlook negative traits or habits when we are in love?

_____

_____

_____

_____

_____

_____

_____

Write about something you let someone get away with because you loved them.

_____

_____

_____

_____

_____

_____

CHAPTER 16
GIRL 2: UNSURE

I married Elijah when I was 22 years old. I knew I didn't love him, but my parents said I needed to marry a good man and all my problems would go away. He's not the worst husband, and he blessed me with two children that are the loves of my life, but I still don't love him.

Elijah will one day pastor a well-known church here in the city, and he'll need a queen by his side to set the example of a godly marriage. And I want so badly to avoid my parents' disappointment, because unlike me, they truly love Elijah. Not only that, leaving him would break up the home we've made for our children. I'm left with a choice. Do I sacrifice my happiness for the fantasy life from which I desperately want to escape, or do I place my happiness above all and deal with damage the breakup will cause my church, my children, and my parents for the rest of my life?

Some may think it is best to leave and start over. I can do that, but the biggest challenge I'll face is that I want to start over with a woman. Yes, I'm a lesbian. Deep down I know this, and my husband knows it too. I've been fighting it since before we were married. I don't want to be a lesbian, but I know that I am, and I need therapy.

When I was young, I knew I was different. All the girls around me were crushing on the cute guys, and although I thought they were cute too, I didn't fantasize about them at all. When my friends thought Taye Diggs and Morris Chestnut were hot, I would laugh and go along with it, but inside I was really thinking about Meagan Good and Gabrielle Union. I didn't experiment with my sexuality until college—mainly because I was afraid, but also because I was sure I was a lesbian. And surely my parents wouldn't be supportive, so I had to wait until there was no way they would find out.

The first time I tried sex with a guy, it was to be sure I was a lesbian. It was the night of my senior prom, and I did the do with Elijah. He was attractive, but I wasn't that into him. He went to my church and my parents had marked him a good guy, so when he asked me to prom I said *yes*. He was a gentleman, and after prom, he asked if I was ready to go home.

"No, not really."

"You want to get something to eat?"

"I'm not hungry."

"What would you like to do?"

I looked at him with an expression that said, "You tryna get these draws?" He seemed to catch my drift.

"You wanna go to Wolfcreek View?" he asked.

Wolfcreek was a spot in the cut where teenagers would go to make out. I had never been before, but everyone knew about it.

"Sure."

He wasn't a virgin, but he didn't have much experience. We did it in the back seat of his car, and it was just okay. It wasn't an experience I was eager have again. It wasn't him though, it was me. I wasn't interested, but he seemed to have a great time. His ass was in love and asked to make it official, but I told him that since we were heading off to different colleges, it would be pointless. We agreed to hangout over the summer, and that was fun. We even did it once more, and it was better than prom night. This time, he ate me out and I enjoyed it way better than penetration, but still didn't cum. That August, we both left for school and didn't talk much.

Freshman year, I started hanging out with Alexis. She was bi and beautiful. She looked like a girl in a magazine. She walked right over to me in the student union and said, "Yo, let's hang out."

I was so distracted by her beauty that I initially couldn't find the words to respond. I mustered, "Who me?"

"Yeah, freshman. No one else is sitting here."

I don't know if I was attracted to her or afraid of her. She had a gentle forcefulness that was magnetic.

I said, "Okay, cool."

We exchanged numbers and started hanging out that night. We started at a party and then stopped for breakfast around 3 AM. While eating her scrambled eggs, she casually asked, "So, you into studs or fem for fem action?"

152 | AISHA HOLLAND DUDLEY & TRE FLOYD

Confusion was plastered on my face. "Excuse me?"

She said, "Girl, it's obvious you're a lesbian. I want to know what type of girls you're into."

I didn't know how to answer. One, I couldn't figure out how she clocked me, and two, I didn't know the lingo.

"Honestly, I don't know. But how did you know?"

"How did I know I was gay or how did I know you were gay?"

"Both, I guess."

"Well, I've known about me since I was a child. I'm bi though. I enjoy a little dick every now and then. I prefer to identify as lesbian. Bi sounds so freaky to me."

"Okay. And how did you know I was a lesbian— which I'm not completely sure I am?"

"Gay knows gay, girl. I can just tell. You're a virgin too, huh?"

"No, I'm not!"

"Maybe not with a guy, but you are with a girl. Are you trying to wait for that special someone or are you just too scared to try it?"

"Maybe I'm just too scared."

"You find me attractive?"

"I do."

"You wanna fuck?"

"I think so."

She was so free—like she had not a care in the world. How could she just ask me that? It was intriguing, and I wanted her, but I also wanted to be her.

We went back to her dorm room since she didn't have a roommate, and she ate me from dawn to dusk. It was the best experience I had ever had. It was nothing like prom with Elijah, or even the night he went down on me. The next morning, we did it again. This time, she taught me how to eat a girl. It took a minute, but I finally got it. She was a great teacher, and I made her cum all over my face. After we cleaned up, I found myself staring at her.

"What does this mean?" I asked.

She said, "What do you mean?"

"Do we date now? Are we dating?"

"No. I mean—you want to date me?"

"I don't know."

"I don't think we should. You're cool, but I think we should be friends. Besides, you're a freshman. You need to explore a little more. You don't need to date anyone right now."

Her response was fine with me because I didn't want to be a lesbian anyway. I said, "You're right."

"Cool. Now let's go get lunch."

She was so cool. We had just had sex, and we were heading out for lunch like it was nothing. Before long, I found myself in gay bars, sleeping with different girls and spiraling into the gay lifestyle. I wanted to sleep with every girl I met and was horny all the time. It effected every part of me, and my grades started to slip. Alexis told me that I needed to slow down. She supported me doing me but insisted that I didn't have to *do* everyone. She suggested that I take a breather, so I decided it was time I went home for a weekend.

While at home, I visited my old church. That Sunday, it was as if Pastor Brown was preaching directly to me. He talked about how homosexuality is a sin, and I sat and cried. I believe my mom became aware in that moment, because she kept looking over at me. After service, she asked when I last talked to Elijah, and I told her that I hadn't talked to him in a while. She insisted we talk. Before we headed out, I went over to Elijah, who still played drums at the church. There was a little small talk, and our natural friendliness was still there. So, when he asked me to dinner, I obliged.

After dinner, I went back to my parents' house before returning to campus. My mom asked about my time with Elijah, and I told her that it was fine. When I started to update her on my experience at school, I must've mentioned Alexis' name one too many times.

"Who is this Alexis girl?"

"She's just a friend from school."

"Does she have a boyfriend?"

"No, not that I know of."

"Do you have a boyfriend?"

"No, Mom."

"Why were you crying in church today? What's weighing on you, baby?"

"I don't know. It was a good message, I guess."

"It wasn't that good. Is this Alexis girl gay?"

"Huh? Why would you think that?"

"Well…is she?"

"Maybe. I don't know."

"Has she been pressuring you?"

"No."

"You sure? You been having unnatural thoughts? Are you sleeping with this Alexis girl?"

I must have looked guilty, because she knew instantly, and Mom was furious. No daughter of hers would do such a thing, and she demanded that I not speak to Alexis again. She even made me move out of the dorm and commute to school each day. My freedom was stripped from me, and it felt as if I was back in high school. I had to go to church on Sundays, bible study on Wednesdays, and attend noon-day prayer. She wanted to confide in Pastor about what was going on but was too ashamed. She simply told Pastor to pray that I found my way in college because it was so worldly.

My high school friends had gone away to college, and Elijah was the only person left to engage with socially. So, I confided in him. Mom liked me with Elijah. I don't know if she thought he was a good person, or if she wanted me with a man, or if she just wanted the congregation to see me with one.

When I went out with Elijah after church one day, he knew something wasn't right with me.

"What's up with you?" he asked.

"What do you mean?"

"You've always been different, but there's something else. What's on your mind?"

"I miss my friends and school. That's all."

"I get that. How about we go visit?"

"I can't. My mom would kill me. Not to mention she took my car, so I have no way there."

"I have a car. Let's go."

Elijah and I headed to campus, and I was so excited to see Alexis that what I would tell Elijah when we got there hadn't crossed my mind. Once we got to Alexis's dorm, it was time that I told him.

"Elijah, there's something I need to say."

"What's up?"

"You have to promise not to tell anyone."

"I promise."

"Elijah, I may be a lesbian."

"You *may* be?"

"I think I am."

"Really? What makes you think that?"

"I slept with a girl. That's why my mom made me move back home."

"You're in college. I understand you're probably trying things out."

"It wasn't just one girl."

"Well, I'm sure it's just a phase. We'll pray and it'll be fine. I promise not to tell anyone, and I love you regardless."

Right then, Elijah was my best friend. I didn't know how he would respond, but I appreciated him. We went up to Alexis' room, and she was so happy to see me. We stayed for hours. When Mom called, I told her I was with Elijah, and that we were spending time together. He took the phone and told Mom he was taking good care of me and promised to get me home safely. He didn't tell her where we were, and mom was fine since I was with Elijah.

Alexis thought Elijah was cool, slightly lame, but she enjoyed him. She asked if we wanted to go out, and I wanted to, but I knew it would be a gay adventure and figured Elijah wouldn't want to go. To my surprise, Elijah said, "Sure, I'll go."

"You aren't afraid of a guy trying to hit on you?" I asked.

"If they do, I'll just tell them I'm straight. I'm confident in my sexuality…unlike you," he said with a smile.

We burst out laughing. For Elijah to joke about my sexuality was beyond me, but it made me feel accepted. Who would have thought? It did cross my mind that he may have been DL gay, but I wasn't sure.

The club was cool. Elijah caught the attention of a few guys, but none were disrespectful. While we were at the club, Alexis whispered, "I'm horny" into my ear. I couldn't lie, I was too. I hadn't had any in months.

"Me too, but what about Elijah?"

"What about him?"

"I can't just leave him."

"So, we'll bring him with us."

Was she proposing a threesome? I didn't know if I was ready for that, but Alexis was so persuasive. Before I could stop her, she walked over to Elijah and said, "You think I'm sexy?"

"Hell yeah," he said.

"You would bone, huh?"

"In a heartbeat."

"Church boys. Y'all swear y'all so good but it's a lot of hell in you. So, tell me, you ever had a threesome?"

"Nah."

She looked over at me and then kissed me in front of Elijah. I could see his heart beating through his chest. He was nervous, but slightly turned on too.

Alexis said, "Let's go."

We went back to her dorm room, and I had my first threesome. Elijah had the time of his life. It must have really turned him on because when I let him inside me, he was rock hard. His stroke was better than it was in high school, and this time, he made me cum. We went at it for hours before I remembered I still lived with my mom, and it was 2 AM.

Elijah drove me home, and we talked and laughed the entire drive. It was the best night of our lives. I knew Mom would kill me, but he told me not to worry and that he would protect me. A light in the house was on, so I knew Mom was awake. Elijah walked me to the door and explained to her that it was all his fault. He said he had me out so late because he was talking and praying with me because he needed to be sure.

Mom said, "Be sure about what?"

I was so nervous. My heart started pounding. Was he about to say he needed to be sure I was gay? Seriously? After our threesome, was he going to rat me out?

He said, "I needed to be sure your daughter was the one before I asked for her hand in marriage."

The anger in Mom's eyes went away and my nervousness turned to shock. I wanted him to save my ass, but damn.

Mom cried and said she would love for him to be her son-in-law and that the Lord had answered her prayers. Elijah kissed me on the cheek and left. I didn't know what to think. Mom was so excited, and I was grateful for Elijah, but I didn't want to marry him.

The next day, Elijah called. He said I didn't have to marry him, but he just knew his proposal would get my mom off my back. However, he was open to us getting married. He told me that he loved me and enjoyed our friendship. He wanted a best friend for a wife.

After Elijah (sort of) proposed, Mom swore I had been delivered, so she let me go back to school. Elijah and I grew closer, and we talked all the time. Sometimes he would come on campus and hang out. By then, I had slowed down on the sexcapades and focused on school. I had a girlfriend for a little while, but senior year I started to think long term. I wanted kids, a traditional wedding, and I wanted a husband. So, perhaps Elijah was right. Maybe it was just a phase.

After I graduated and had been working a few years, Mom rehashed the idea of getting married. She said I wouldn't be young forever, and that Elijah wouldn't wait for long. Jokingly, I expressed her concerns to Elijah, and he pulled out a ring. He said he had purchased it a while back and had never stopped loving me. He asked if I would have him as my husband.

I said, "Yes." My affirming response was not because I loved him romantically, but because I loved our friendship. He never told my secrets, and he never judged me. I believe he knew I didn't love him because on our wedding night, he said he wanted to please all of me and invited a girl to our hotel suite. I don't know if it was really for me or for him, but it was good! I hadn't had my girl-itch scratched for a while, and I needed it.

Elijah and I have been married for years now. He's still a great friend. We engage in threesomes on occasion, and we both enjoy it, but they're not enough for me anymore.

Elijah continues to play the drums at church, so I'm forced to hear Pastor condemn homosexuals. He knows

I hate it, but he refuses to leave and says we have to endure it. I'm forced to sit in anti-gay conversations knowing fully well what I desire. The older I get, the more exhausting living this lie becomes. I just can't be sure where I'd land if I decided to leave. I need therapy.

Chapter Sixteen Reflection

Write about a time you put someone else's happiness before your own.

CHAPTER 17
GIRL 1: IT GIRL

Call me Girl 1. I've always been number one in the pretty category. For as long as I can remember, I was told, "You're so pretty," or "You're so cute." I would never hear, "You're so smart," or "Go to college and be a doctor." In most people's eyes, I was destined to be a silent model or dangling from a man's arm as his trophy wife. When I started to believe their limited vision of me, there was no need to focus on the inner work. I invested solely into my image and kept my hair and nails done, dressed chic and fashionable, and stayed fit. Now, I need therapy.

I did meet "the guy," but I was no trophy wife. My need for therapy doesn't stem solely from what I allowed him to do to me. I needed it long before that. Honestly, I've always been a little insecure—okay, majorly insecure. No one would know because I was *that girl* on the outside, but inside, I was a scared little girl who always needed someone to say, "You're so pretty" to validate me.

Adolescent and teenage years were filled with beauty pageants and talent competitions. I won them all. My talent is undeniable, but my wins were mostly achieved because of my beauty. The audience always adored me.

In my 20s, I never paid for a drink at the bar. Between the bartender, random guys, and even a few girls here and there, someone would always cover my tab. I never intended to give any of them the time of day, but a free drink is a free drink.

Every guy wanted to be with me, and in my late 20s, I decided I wanted to be with someone as well. You must understand, when I say I was always that girl...I was always that bitch—long hair, nice skin, and more curves than a rollercoaster. Perhaps I was an emotional rollercoaster, but a rollercoaster, nonetheless. I could have just about any man I wanted and just about every man wanted me—tall ones, fine ones. Hell, even gay ones wanted to be me.

When I met Bryce Bentley, he didn't drive a Bentley, but the brother was fine—tattoos, money in his pocket. He was the type of brother that could hold it down in the street, but you could still take him home to your mom and hold a conversation. Chile, I fell head over heels. He was everything that I was, but in guy form. He was tall, handsome, and could turn heads faster than I could. I was the "it" girl and he was the "it" guy, so naturally we were made for each other.

We dated for two years before he finally popped the question, and we had the wedding of all weddings. Think of the Tyler Perry movie where the angels were suspended from the ceiling. Listen, my wedding made that one look cheap. We were in Essence Magazine, and I'm not even a celebrity.

After dissing a countless number of men who tried to get with me over the years, I was finally with the guy I would be with for life. I was his and he was mine. We were definitely the "it" couple. It seems that everyone posted us on Instagram, Facebook, and blogs. We had a whole TikTok challenge. I was that bitch, and everyone wanted what I had. We were happy. I knew what he liked. He knew what I liked. We would even go to church together. I knew God had blessed me with the perfect man. I had everything.

The thing I didn't know was that everyone else had him too. After a few years, people started to hit me up on social media to ask if Bryce was my man, and I immediately knew what that meant. It meant that he had been seen with someone, or that someone had posted an image of him, but I defended him. Soon after, my friends came to me with receipts—hard evidence receipts.

I'll never forget the day a friend of mine came over. She started with, "I couldn't say this over the phone because you're my girl…" and I instantly knew what she would say, but I indulged her. She presented me with pictures of Bryce and another woman in a hotel room. There were also screenshots of text messages. He wasn't just screwing with some girl; he was having a full-blown affair. On the inside I was falling apart, but outside I held it together. How could he do this to me? The girl wasn't even prettier than me.

My friend was there to comfort me and to listen—I'm sure—but I had to ask why she would even bring it to me. Her look said, "Because I love you, and you can't be this dumb." Her mouth said, "You need to know this. You're my girl, and you deserve better." I told her that Bryce and I would work it out and I thanked her for coming over. It was imperative that I pulled myself together before Bryce came home, so she had to go. When she asked what I planned to do, I told her I'd call her later and let her know.

"Right now, I just need to think," I told her.

She knew I was happy, so I couldn't help but wonder why she would spread rumors. Okay, maybe they weren't rumors. Sure, they all had so-called proof, but Bryce was my man, and I was that girl. I'm not the type of girl who gets cheated on, so why would she bring that to my house? Damn. Who was I kidding? She wasn't the one in the wrong. I couldn't be mad at her when she was trying to be a good friend. I was just too embarrassed to accept the truth. So, I had to decide if I should go off, leave, or stay.

I couldn't leave. Leaving would mean losing, and I've never lost a damn thing—especially a guy. How could I tell people that I'm divorcing him because he was cheating on me? It just didn't fit my personal narrative. I decided I'd talk to him about it, and when I did, he used reverse psychology and made me believe that I was the problem. He said he only cheats because I don't handle him like he needs to be handled and that I don't take good care of him. That was bullshit, and he knew it. I knew it too, but for whatever reason, I couldn't get over him.

When I would leave, I wouldn't be gone too long before someone would ask, "Where is that fine man of yours?" and drive me right back. Don't judge me. As much as I wanted to, I just couldn't say, "You mean that fine man of mine that was cheating on me?" That would make *me* look bad, and I refused to look desperate and rejected. It has never been my style. So, I would respond by saying that he was at home, and that I was headed there myself, which left me with only the last option. I had to stay. I may not be the happiest, but it's better than not having a man. Seriously, I'm just not that girl. I don't jump from one failed relationship to the next and sleep with man after man. I was taught to hold my man down. I figured if I just prayed and kept myself fixed up, he would eventually stop.

I think he stopped for a little while, but it was already too late. When everyone already knows your business, it haunts you. I still had to deal with stares and side eyes from those who assumed he was still cheating. It was our bed, and we were going to lay in it together. That is, until what should have been the final straw.

One day in early spring, I looked out my work window, and it was beautiful. Since I was practically done for the day, I decided to go for a run. I went home to change into my running clothes and noticed Bryce's car. I thought it was strange, but perhaps he had come home for lunch. I walked into the house and called his name.

"Bryce! Are you home? Bryce?"

"Hey, baby. I'm up here."

He was in the bedroom without a shirt on his body and was buckling up his pants.

"Baby, what are you doing at home in the middle of the day? And why are you half dressed?"

"I had a long morning, so I took a half day. I just got out of the shower."

"Oh okay. It's such a nice day outside that I decided to take a half day too. I planned to go for a run, but since you're off, maybe we can spend the day together."

"Nah, bae, you go on your run. I'm just going to relax."

"Well, I'll chill with you."

"Nah, you go ahead. We can chill later."

That's when I assumed something was up, but I was going to play along.

I said, "Okay, let me change and I'll be on my way. Where are my tennis shoes?" I kneeled to look beneath the bed when he stopped me.

"Baby, can you make me a sandwich?"

"Sure! Let me change first."

"Nah, let's just go out to eat."

"But you said you wanted to relax. Baby, what is going on?"

"I don't want you to look under the bed because I have a surprise for you. That's why I'm home early. I went to pick it up and hid it, and I don't want you to see it yet."

My suspicion faded. When I thought he had someone in the house, he was actually doing something sweet for me—until I heard someone sneeze.

"Bitch, come out from under the bed!"

Some random bitch came from underneath the bed butt ass naked.

"Well, I guess you forgot to wrap my surprise. How the fuck could you? In my house! In my bed! I should kill both y'all asses!"

I ran into to the closet, and he knew exactly what would be in hand when I returned—my gun. He tried to get her scary ass to run as he tried to calm me down.

"Ain't no *calm down*!"

When I started firing down the stairs, she ran full speed out my front door butt ass naked. I don't know where she went or how she got there, and I couldn't care less.

"How could you, Bryce?"

"It's not you, it's me."

"I know that, asshole. You gotta go."

"Don't put me out, baby."

"You put yourself out. In my house? In my bed? I can't. That's some low shit—even for you."

"Baby, I'll go to counseling. Just don't leave me."

He cried and fell to his knees. I had never seen him in such a vulnerable state. It was like previous times that he was caught lying to me, but there was something about this time that seemed genuine. And like a fool, I let him stay, and we went to counseling. We talked, and it seemed to help. We appeared happy again, but before long I started to see the same old signs. I found receipts to strip clubs and would smell perfume on his clothes. I knew what was up, but I just didn't have the strength to leave. I had stayed through so much shit; I figured it would be pointless to leave now.

Whenever a woman calls my house or whispers behind my back, I remind myself that at least I have a man. What do they have? If they would stop trying to sleep with my man, I wouldn't have this problem. So yes, he's my man and I'm sticking beside him. Sure, we have our problems, but point out a perfect couple that doesn't. At least my man's not going upside my head, and he ain't broke. He ain't got kids all over town. Regardless, bitches are still jealous of me. I will always be his number one...even if it is a damn lie.

Hearing myself say it aloud lets me know that it's not him, it's me. I just don't know how to let him go. I was always told that I was beautiful, so I never focused on learning life skills. I won every contest I entered, but I can't seem to win myself back from this guy. I could never see my competition, and now it's as if I'm in competition for my own husband...and I'm losing. I could walk away and still win in life, but my insecurities won't allow me to do it. I may not know what to do about my marriage, but I do know that I need therapy.

Chapter Seventeen Reflection

What insecurities do you possess that need your attention?

_____

_____

_____

_____

_____

_____

_____

CHAPTER 18
GIRL .5: ALMOST

Who said it was impossible to miss what you never had? When I think about it, I never almost had you. Were you ever mine? Will you always be mine? Who am I? How can we celebrate love that happens too late and how can I say the words I'm about to say? I'm number .5, or ½, as I'm only halfway in this marriage, and I need therapy.

I've been married to Brandon for two years. Brandon is a great guy and has all the qualities a girl could want in a man. He sends me flowers, opens doors, has a great job, listens, makes me feel protected, and makes me feel secure in every way. Brandon is not the problem. Jackson is the problem. Actually, Jackson is not the problem. I'm the problem because I can't get my mind off Jackson.

Three years ago, my girl, Alicia, set me up on a blind date with Jackson. I had been single for a while, and she thought it was time that I got back out there. I agreed, but on the night of our date, I flaked. There was some work that needed my attention, so I used it as an excuse. Honestly, I was just nervous and quite skeptical about a blind date. I wasn't desperate and I didn't feel like faking it through a conversation if I wasn't interested. When I told Alicia I couldn't make it, she emphasized how much I was missing out. And I said I'd somehow get over it.

Two months after the curved blind date, I'm engaged in work at a nearby coffee shop when I noticed a fly, bald brother sitting in the common area talking to two other guys. I overheard their discussion on a hair investment project but tried not to listen. However, I was intrigued. Then the fine brother walked over to my table.

"Hi, ma'am."

"Hello."

"I see you're working, but might I borrow you for a quick moment?"

Instinct said to tell him I was busy, as I was sure this was a ploy to get my attention but—to be honest—he already had my attention.

I responded, "How can I help?"

"These gentlemen are trying to get me to invest in a hair care product. As you can see, I have no hair. But you have beautiful locks, and I was wondering if you could share your thoughts."

"I'm not sure about investments, but I can give my opinion on hair care."

I joined the conversation, and before I knew it, we had been talking for two hours. It started quite professionally. After 30 minutes, and with my expertise in Black hair, he decided that the product would be of no benefit to his portfolio. Afterwards, the other gentlemen left, and the two of us engaged in great conversation.

"I've really enjoyed talking with you. Thanks for your advice; that would've cost me a lot of money. Do you frequent here?"

"You're quite welcome. I come here from time to time. It's near my building."

"Oh, you live in the TEN building? My cousin, Alicia, lives there."

"I know Alicia. What did you say your name was?"

"Jackson."

"So…crazy question. Did she try to set you up on a blind date about two months ago?"

"Yeah, she did, but the girl didn't show. I felt dumb because I wasn't going to go initially. And then she didn't even show."

"Wow. That's crazy."

"What? Don't tell me you're the girl."

"That would be me. This is awkward."

"Wow! That's crazy."

"That's what I said."

Inside, I thought, "Girl, you missed out on this fine ass brother," but I couldn't say it aloud. Instead, I said, "Well, since it's not a blind date anymore, and you owe me 10% for my consulting here today, perhaps we can go on an official date some time."

"10%, huh? I thought this was a free consultation. Sheesh! I would actually love to go on a date, but I recently started seeing someone, so…"

"Understood."

I felt like an idiot. Why didn't Alicia tell me her cousin was this fine? Not to mention, he's intelligent and can hold a conversation. I felt that my future husband was right in front of me, but he was going off to see someone else.

"I guess I should go. It was nice meeting you. Perhaps we'll meet again," he said as he left.

I immediately called Alicia and she told me that it was all my fault, and that I should have listened to her in the first place. She was right, but oh well. I can't miss something I never had. Or can I?

Three months later, I met Brandon. We met at the same coffee house near my condo. And if I am being honest, I always hoped Jackson would come by and say that he was single again. To my surprise, it was Brandon.

Brandon had recently moved to Atlanta and was shopping for the perfect condo when he stopped in for a quick bite. We started up a conversation, and he told me that TEN was amongst his top choices. I let him know that it was a nice spot, and he asked if he'd get to see me more if he moved into the building. It was a cute line, so I smiled, and we exchanged numbers. He signed a lease on a unit two floors above mine. Had we known then, he could have just moved in with me because he was always at my spot, or I was at his. Brandon is everything I could've asked for in a man, and we dated exclusively for nearly a year.

On my morning jog through Piedmont Park, I stopped to take a breather near the gazebo when I heard a familiar voice say, "Well, well, look who it is."

I turned to see Jackson standing there sweaty and shirtless. Sweat dripped from his bald head, and his skin glistened like a popsicle melting from a stick on a hot Atlanta day.

"Fancy seeing you here."

He told me that he usually runs at Grant Park but decided to do something different. We talked for a while. As I was about to leave, he asked if I was seeing anyone, and if we could get coffee sometime. It was déjà vu all over again. I explained that I had been dating and asked about the girl he was seeing the last time we met. Things hadn't worked out between them, and he was mad at himself for not going out with me after we met at the coffee house. He felt he had missed an opportunity with someone who could have been his wife. Was this guy playing with me? Did he know I felt the same way? How could he have known that? *Ugh!* Whoever said it's impossible to miss what you never had clearly had never almost had Jackson.

"The last time, you were dating. This time, I'm dating. Who knows...the next time we see each other, maybe we'll both be available," I said with a bright smile. I didn't think much of it, and planned to walk away, but his response shook me.

"If you think we will be available next time, why don't we just make ourselves available now?"

"Huh?"

"If you think you'll be available later, it's possible you don't see a future with this guy. Let's not waste any more time and see what this could be."

It shook me to my core. Was he right? If I was truly in love with Brandon, would I have said that? Did I already see the end of me and Brandon? Should I go ahead and end it with him? I couldn't. Brandon was everything and I'd only had a few encounters with Jackson. I would be an idiot to stop seeing Brandon to take a chance on Jackson.

"Jackson, I can't. As tempting as it sounds, I can't."

"You can't or you won't? I'm sorry to put you in this position but I should have taken a chance on you. Don't make the same mistake I did. Take a chance on me."

"I'm sorry, Jackson. I can't."

I continued my jog and left him near the gazebo, but I thought of him the entire way back. Had I made a big mistake? Why did I fancy this guy so much? I told myself to forget about him. Brandon was right in front of me, tried and true, and I needed to focus on him.

When I returned to my apartment, the floor was covered in roses. My living room looked like a scene from a movie, and a trail of flowers led to the bedroom, so I expected to see Brandon down on one knee. Sure enough, there was Brandon, a few of my girlfriends, my parents and his homeboys.

"Baby, I know you hate surprises, but I wanted this moment to be special. We've been together for almost a year, and I don't want to call you my girlfriend any longer. I want you to be my wife. Will you let me be your husband?"

I had just spent the last hour thinking about a man whose last name I didn't even know, and this man was ready to make me his wife. His proposal was all the assurance I needed. I can't miss something I never had, and Brandon was what I wanted and needed.

"Yes! Yes, I'll be your wife."

Brandon and I had a beautiful ceremony with our closest friends and family. Since that day, and even before that day, he has been the perfect guy. I love him so much. Brandon and I are on such good terms that we have given thought to expanding our family and having children. I hadn't thought about Jackson much at all until a few days ago when I had to go to DC for a work conference. Lo and behold, guess who was there. Jackson. We spotted each other at the conference registration, and he walked over to me looking as amazing as always.

"Well, if it isn't you. You look beautiful."

"You look good as well. I didn't expect to see you here."

"I didn't expect to be here either, but I invested in this company when it was just a start up."

"Wow! My firm does the marketing for the company."

"Small world."

"How have you been?"

"I've been well. I'm married now."

"Congratulations to you. Is it Brandon?"

"It is. How are you? Some lucky girl scooped you up yet?"

"As a matter of fact, yes. I'm engaged and plan to be married next week."

"Well, congrats to you and your bride."

I quickly, but not too quickly, turned and walked away. Hearing that he would soon be married triggered me. And all the hopeful thought about him—about us—came flooding back. All my doubts about Brandon came back too. Had I made the right decision? Was I on the right path? Should I have chosen Jackson? I wasn't unhappy with Brandon, but there's something about the road not taken that haunted me.

After the conference that evening, I decided to go to the bar at the host hotel. I knew Jackson would be there, or at least I hoped he would be. Sure enough, he was. I walked up to him wearing a dress I had bought at the hotel's boutique that showed every curve I had and then some.

"Well, well. Join me for a drink?"

"I'd love to, Jackson."

"So, let's just cut to it."

"Cut to what?"

"I saw that dress in the boutique window. You bought it just so you could wear it down here and show me how beautiful you look in it."

"What? That's nonsense. I already had this dress." I was lying through my teeth.

"Sure, you did. The thing is, I don't need to see you in a nice dress. You're always beautiful, but why did you feel the need to put it on?"

"Ugh! I don't know. I guess I was just…"

"Wondering about the road not traveled?"

"Yes. How did you know?"

"I ask Alicia about you all the time. And I kept waiting for you and Brandon to break up, but you never did. I wanted to be respectful, but I also wanted a chance. Honestly, I knew the very day you got married."

"You did?"

"Alicia was in your wedding, right? Sorry for pretending I didn't know."

"Wow."

"But listen, your level of commitment to him finally caused me to give up. I was just glad that you were happy. You *are* happy, right?"

"I am. I just can't help but wonder if I'd be happier if I had gone on that initial blind date."

"Well, we're here in DC. No fiancé, no Brandon. I'm not saying we should do anything, but I don't know if we will have this moment again."

"I don't know if we should."

"I'm in room 905 if you decide we should spend an evening together. Sex is not a requirement. We can just hold each other and see how that road would have been. Finally get it out of our systems forever."

"I'll consider."

"I'll be waiting." He grabbed his jacket and proceeded out the bar.

I waited another five minutes and then went to my room. What to do? I knew that if I went to his room, there would be more than *holding* taking place.

I took a shower, laced myself in perfume and decided to call my husband. We sat on the phone for hours. Ultimately, I fell asleep. When I awoke around 4 AM, I thought I should knock on Jackson's door. I put on my robe and walked down the hall, but I couldn't bring myself to knock. As I walked back to the elevator, I heard a door opening, and I dared not turn around. It could have been a co-worker and there would be no way to explain.

The next morning, as I checked out of the hotel, I saw Jackson. He smiled and didn't make a big deal in front of the concierge.

As we both awaited our rides to the airport, he leaned over to me and said, "Just couldn't bring yourself to knock, huh? I opened the door and saw you walking away. It's okay that you couldn't knock. I couldn't make myself come down the hall after you either. I guess we'll never know what we never had." As his Uber arrived, he turned and said, "If you are ever in LA, hit me up."

That was the last time I saw Jackson, but I think of him all the time—sometimes while I'm alone, and sometimes while I'm with Brandon. I often contemplate going to LA, but I never do. It's not fair to Brandon that I have these thoughts, but I don't know how to make them go away. Should I do it and see what happens, or just be plagued by these thoughts forever? Am I fully giving myself to Brandon if I continue to have these thoughts? I don't know. That's why I need therapy.

Chapter Eighteen Reflection

Have you ever missed something that you never truly had?

_____
_____
_____
_____
_____
_____
_____

Is the wonder of not knowing what could have been worse than doing something you know you will regret?

_____
_____
_____
_____
_____
_____
_____

EPILOGUE

Therapy was not always a popular topic, but we live in a time that many of us are waking up to its benefits. Like the women in these pages, we are all in need of guidance, clarity and healing, and counseling is a great method to achieve it. It is time to confront the darkness and take back your power.

No one ever promised that life would be easy but recognize the tools that are available to help you navigate it. If life is anything less than perfect, you may benefit from new perspective and insight that comes from digging deep into who you are, what you desire, and why you desire it. Refuse to suppress the real you and walk in the light of your truth.

Until next time, girls…

XOXO

ABOUT THE AUTHORS

Aisha Holland Dudley is a native of Coffeeville, MS. She attended Mississippi State University where she received a bachelor's degree in Speech Communication. Aisha began her career as a speech/debate coach at a high school in Texas. She has always had a passion for public speaking and is excited to use her gift to share this book with the world. After traveling with her husband, Emanuel, for over 20 years while he served in the military, they moved to the Atlanta, GA area after his retirement. Aisha is very proud of her two children, Devin and Meagan. She enjoys her current position running the daily business of Tre Productions, the first black-owned theater in Forest Park, GA.

Tre Floyd is a native of Mississippi and has been in some form of the arts since childhood. He acted in church plays and sang in local talent shows as a young child. While pursuing a degree in Accounting (and graduating with honors), Tre also learned about stage and film within his Theatre Arts minor. He has trained dancers and performed at various venues across the US, both acting and dancing. Tre Floyd is the owner of Tre's Place Theater just outside of Atlanta, GA. It's currently the only theater in the city of Forest Park. Tre is known for writing and directing stage plays such as *Love, Sex & Marriage*, *Before Black Lives Matter*, *Dear John*, *She Got It*, and more. Tre has toured stage performances across the USA, selling out stages from Miami to Indianapolis to

Baltimore to Memphis. This is Tre's first book, and he is excited to share it with the world.